Book Two

Monster Problems

By

R.L. Ullman

Monster Problems 2

Cover design by Yusup Mediyan
All character images created with heromachine.com.

Published by But That's Another Story... Press
Ridgefield, CT

Printed in the United States of America.

First Printing, 2020.

ISBN: 978-1-7340612-4-6
Library of Congress Control Number: 2020905528

To Marge,
thanks for watching over us

TABLE OF CONTENTS

CHAPTER ONE

BLIND AS A BAT

"**C**ome on, Brampire!" comes a voice from behind me.

Based on the nasally tone, it sounded like Rage.

"You've got this!" comes another voice.

That's definitely Aura.

"If you lose, you're a moron!"

And there's good old InvisiBill.

Well, I guess people have different ideas of what they consider motivating. But it doesn't really matter what they say because I've got all the self-motivation I need. After all, my entire team is counting on me not to blow it.

I look across the gym at my opponent, a bubbling mass of kid-flesh codenamed Blobby. His real name is Bobby Rotunda, and he's essentially a blob—a boneless, amorphous pile of goop categorized as an 'abnormal,' also known as a one-of-a-kind monster.

He easily weighs over a thousand pounds and is best known for gobbling up everything and anything in sight, which could include me if I'm not careful. At the moment, he's cheating ever-so-slightly, rolling inch-after-inch of his skin over the starting line.

I guess I could complain but I'm not too worried about it. I mean, I'm pretty confident I could dust him in anything other than a hot dog eating contest. But maybe I'm feeling too confident. After all, this isn't exactly a normal kind of competition.

Nope. It's a monster competition.

More specifically, it's the 42nd annual Monster Cup.

Apparently, the Monster Cup is a pretty big deal around here at the Van Helsing Academy. It's a two-week competition pitting different sections of the academy against one another in a variety of events like races, quizzes, and other spooky shenanigans. Whatever team tallies the most points at the end wins the Monster Cup— a big silver trophy with a tiny skull on top that you can display proudly on your dorm room floor.

Aura has been talking about it nonstop for weeks. Honestly, I don't think I've ever met anyone as competitive as she is. According to her, losing is not an option. So, she's woken us up early every morning before class to grill us on monster trivia and put us through grueling exercise drills. And if you thought getting up at dawn was painful, try standing next to Hairball before he's showered.

G.R.O.S.S.

Anyway, I had hoped the hard work would pay off, but we're currently trailing the Howlers 3-2 in our very first event! But I suppose I shouldn't be too surprised because the Howlers are older than us and have way more experience using their Supernatural powers. There's Blobby, my current opponent, but they also have Harpoon, a green-skinned harpy with wings, Putrid Pete, a decaying mummy, MinoTodd, who is half-minotaur, half-kid, Lucky, a goth guy with a cursed amulet, and Gnatalie, a teeny-tiny girl with big, buggy eyes.

I hate to admit it, but after watching the Howlers in action I have to say they're pretty impressive. But it's not like I can go over and shake their hands, or whatever appendage they offer me. First of all, my fellow Monstrosities would kill me. And second, bragging rights are on the line.

The smack talk between sections has been intense, and if we end up losing this round, the Howlers will tease us like crazy. Fortunately, Aura and Hairball won their heats to keep us in the game. But now it's up to me.

No pressure, right?

I have to win for us to save face and walk out here with at least a tie. And right now, my face, as well as the rest of my body, is in the form of a bat.

I flap my wings, hovering unsteadily behind the starting line. Let's just say that being a bat is something I'm still getting used to. Even though I've practiced a lot, I'm no expert—not by a long shot. And I've noticed I'm developing some really 'bat' habits in my human form, like the urge to hang upside down and just chill.

"Mr. Murray!" Professor Hexum barks. "Focus!"

One

I snap back to reality.

Looking down, I see Hexum's green eyes glaring back up at me. His eyebrows are furrowed and he's leaning forward on his walking stick, gripping it so tightly his knuckles are white. He's clearly not happy with me.

Surprise, surprise.

Ever since I came to the Van Helsing Academy, Hexum has been a major thorn in my side. He claims he's doing it to make me stronger, but I'm finding that increasingly hard to believe. In fact, torturing me seems to be his favorite pastime. Like now, for instance. For some reason, he's forcing me to compete only as a bat while everyone else got to compete in any way they wanted.

It's just not fair.

"Attention racers!" Hexum calls out. "When I say 'go,' an object will appear in the center of the gymnasium floor. The first one to bring it back to their side—by whatever means necessary—wins."

Um, what? Did he just say, 'by whatever means necessary?' He didn't say that for the other races.

Suddenly, there's a deep RUMBLE and I realize Blobby is laughing. You know, there's something really disturbing about a mountain of giggling flesh.

"You've got this, Bram!" Aura yells.

That's funny, I thought I did too. Right up until now.

"Ready!" Hexum calls out, raising his walking stick into the air. "Set! Go!"

Suddenly, a long, pointed piece of wood appears in

the center of the gym floor and I do a double take. Um, is that what I think it is? Because it sort of looks like a—

"Grab the stake, Bram!" Rage yells.

That is a stake! Like, a stake used to destroy vampires! And the last time I checked, I'm still a vampire. So, why would Hexum ask me to retrieve a—

"Less gawking and more flapping!" Aura yells.

Huh? Well, she's right about that. If I just hang here, we're guaranteed to lose. But I might be too late anyway because, despite Blobby's lack of legs, he's inching closer to the target!

I've got to move!

I figure my best bet is to just swoop down before Blobby gets there and pick up the stake with my feet. It sounds easy enough, but there's just one problem. I'm not so great at the 'swooping' part.

In fact, I'd say my flying skills are downright shaky.

Nevertheless, I have no choice but to go for it, so I angle my body towards the stake, and take off, flapping with all of my might. Within seconds I'm there, but so is Blobby, and he's completely covered the stake with his body, forming an enormous skin-shield.

I try slowing down, but apparently bats don't come with brakes! My head pushes into Blobby's sweaty flesh like I've jumped onto a trampoline, and then it recoils, slinging me skyward!

"I can't watch," I hear Rage say.

"Are you kidding?" InvisiBill says, "This is epic!"

Oh, when I get my fangs in that dufus…

I flap like crazy until I manage to right myself, and then I double back for another try. Except this time the stake is gone! Since Blobby is heading back to his side of the gym, he must be carrying the stake somewhere beneath his undulating body!

If he crosses the finish line, we'll lose!

I can't let that happen, but how can I stop him?

I mean, I'm just a bat.

And then it hits me.

I'm a bat!

That means I can do everything a bat can do—and that includes 'seeing' using sound. One of the more unique things about being a bat is being able to use sonic radar. When I'm flying (or at least, trying to fly) I can make high-frequency sounds that echo off of objects, allowing me to detect things I couldn't see as a regular human being, including the range, size, and shape of a target object.

Time for some radar love!

I sweep around Blobby and project sound waves all around him. Most of them hit his body and ping back, but some hit nothing—and bingo—I've found my opening!

Since Blobby is gelatinous, he's moving by using the folds of his skin to push himself along the ground. So that means at any given time, some parts of him aren't in contact with the floor. If I can slide into one of those pockets, maybe I can reach the stake and grab it from him.

I just need to time this right.

I hover at ground level, waiting for my chance, and when a large fold lifts, I act.

"Bram?" I hear Aura call out. "What are you—?"

But I don't wait for her to finish her sentence, because I dart beneath Blobby into a pocket of air. It's snug in here, and ugh, everything smells like armpit, but I've got a job to do!

Then, I locate my target.

Blobby has the stake beneath him alright, but it's wrapped in a ball of his flesh.

Nasty.

But I can't worry about that now. I just need to grab the stake and get out before my pocket closes. I spin around and latch onto an exposed part of the wood with my feet and attempt to fly out, but Blobby is holding it so tightly I can't pull away!

Then, I feel pressure all around my body. Blobby's skin is closing in on me! My left wing smushes against my side and suddenly I can't fly! Then, my feet slip off the stake! Hexum said to win by any means necessary and Blobby is taking him up on it!

He's trying to crush me!

I look up to see a wall of flesh closing in around my head. I've got to get out of here! I don't care what Hexum said about only competing as a bat!

I muster all of my concentration into one thought.

Be… a mist!

Suddenly, my limbs feel all tingly, and then my body is lighter than air. But as my molecules disperse, I realize I couldn't hold the stake in this form even if I wanted to, so there's no point staying trapped in here. Instead, I focus on pushing my molecules outward, squeezing through the microscopic gaps in Blobby's suffocating mass.

And then, I'm free!

I collect my molecules in the center of the gym floor and focus on becoming a kid again. As I rematerialize on my stomach, covered in flop sweat and breathing heavily, I can only watch as Blobby rumbles across his starting line and the Howlers jump for joy.

We lost. And it's all my fault.

Suddenly, I feel someone standing behind me. It's probably one of my teammates coming over to cheer me up. But when I roll over, all I see is Hexum.

"Your team is disqualified," Hexum says.

"What?" I say, confused. "Why?"

"I gave you strict instructions to compete as a bat," Hexum says. "And you violated those instructions."

"What are you talking about?" I say. "You said to win by whatever means necessary. If I stayed a bat, he would have pulverized me."

"*Your* instructions were to compete as a bat," Hexum says, scribbling on his pad. "And you could have won by whatever means were necessary—as a *bat*. The Monstrosities are disqualified from the tournament. Your team is eliminated from the Monster Cup."

"What?" Aura says, floating over. "But that's ridiculous! Bram was almost killed!"

"Was he?" Hexum says. "He seems fine to me. But I suppose you can view his survival as a positive outcome of your team's disqualification."

"Hardly," InvisiBill says.

"Shut it," Aura says. "This isn't fair. Not to mention that you made his object a stake. We all know that stakes kill vampires. What was that about?"

"I would call it an unfortunate coincidence," Hexum says. "The objects used in this competition are… randomly generated."

"Yeah," I say. "Sure they are."

"Congratulations, Howlers," Hexum says, exiting the gym. "You are moving on. The Monstrosities, however, will now have plenty of time for extra homework."

"This is so unfair," Rage says, crossing his arms.

"Nice try, Monstrosities!" Harpoon calls out as the Howlers leave the gym, giving each other high fives. "But don't feel bad you lost to us, because we're going to win the Monster Cup!"

"I'm sorry, guys," I say, turning to my team. But as I look around, I realize no one is looking back at me. Instead, they're all staring at their shoes. "I didn't try to break the rules."

"Well, that's what you did," InvisiBill says.

"Yeah," Hairball says. "Thanks for nothing."

As the two of them leave, I look over at Stanphibian who shakes his fishbowl-covered head and gives me two webbed thumbs down. Then, he follows them out.

Awesome.

I see Aura floating with her shoulders slumped and I feel awful. I know how much she wanted to win the Monster Cup. She really wanted to prove we were the best section. But thanks to me, now she won't get the chance.

"Hey," I say, as a thought crosses my mind. "Maybe we can appeal Hexum's ruling to Van Helsing? Maybe he'll let us back in the tournament?"

"Yeah," Aura mutters. "Maybe."

And then she turns and vanishes through the wall.

Well, that didn't go well.

"What about you?" I ask Rage. "Are you mad at me too?"

"What?" he says, looking glum. "Um, no."

"Great," I say. "Because—"

But he doesn't bother to hear the rest of my sentence, because he pushes through the gym door. And as it SLAMS shut behind him, the only person left to hear its echo is me.

VAN HELSING ACADEMY

THE MONSTROSITIES

CODENAME:
- Aura

CATEGORY:
- Spirit

TYPE:
- Ghost

CODENAME:
- Brampire

CATEGORY:
- Undead

TYPE:
- Vampire

CODENAME:
- Hairball

CATEGORY:
- Abnormal

TYPE:
- Yeti

Got Monster?

CODENAME:
- Invisi-Bill

CATEGORY:
- Abnormal

TYPE:
- Invisible

CODENAME:
- Rage

CATEORY:
- Abnormal

TYPE:
- Jekyll/Hyde

CODENAME:
- Stan-phibian

CATEGORY:
- Abnormal

TYPE:
- Gill-man

ROLL CALL SHEET

CHAPTER TWO

NEW BLOOD

I've never felt so alone.

And that's saying something considering all of the foster homes and group facilities I've passed through. Growing up I never bothered connecting with anyone because I knew I wouldn't be sticking around. But here I thought I found a place to call home.

I guess I was wrong.

Yes, I single-handedly ruined my team's chances for glory by getting us disqualified from the Monster Cup, but I didn't expect my friends to give me the cold shoulder like this. I mean, I already felt bad enough, but now I feel even worse because nobody came to my room to check up on me—including Rage, my roommate.

But it's probably for the best because I didn't want to see anyone anyway. I pretty much spent the entire afternoon fuming in bed, staring at the ceiling and wishing I was someone else.

Anyone else.

I did get up once to go see Van Helsing, but as soon

as I hit the foyer, I overheard someone saying he was locked in his office, talking to some strange man. That stopped me in my tracks. After all, I know Van Helsing and he doesn't like to be disturbed. So, I marched back upstairs for more fuming.

In fact, I was so upset I even skipped dinner, which I know is a major 'no-no' for a vampire like me. But even though I was hungry, I'd rather starve than see my 'so-called' friends' faces.

I bet they were talking about me anyway. After all, how many boneheaded things could one person do before they get kicked out of here? And I've done some pretty boneheaded things. You know, like resurrecting Count Dracula with my own blood.

I'm pretty sure no one can top that one.

I should probably just leave.

Suddenly, the door bursts open, scaring the bejesus out of me.

"You coming?" Rage asks, poking his head inside.

"Coming where?" I ask, not bothering to look his way. I guess I'm as mad at him as he is of me.

"To the auditorium," he says. "There was an announcement at dinner. Van Helsing called a mandatory assembly for all students and faculty in the auditorium. He expects everyone to be there, including you."

"Not me," I say. "I'll be right here."

"That's ridiculous," Rage says. "You have to go. Van Helsing never calls a mandatory assembly. Supposedly, this is the first time in years that's happened. Are you really going to miss it?"

"Yep," I say. "I don't need to hear anything else about the Monster Cup. It's pretty clear where we are in the standings, which is nowhere, all because of me."

"This assembly isn't about the Monster Cup," Rage says. "And besides, I'm not mad anymore. What happened wasn't your fault. You had a bad break, that's all. No one wanted you to die so we could win. Well, except for InvisiBill."

"Really?" I say, looking at him.

He's smiling and I can't help but smile back.

"What about Aura?" I ask.

"Don't worry about her," Rage says. "She'll get over it. Eventually. Now get up or we'll be late."

I hesitate for a second, but I am curious about why Van Helsing called this assembly. "Fine," I say, throwing my legs over the side of the bed. I grab my gray hoodie and follow Rage outside.

There's a full moon in the night sky as groups of kids make their way across the green towards the main building. Rage and I are the last to climb up the stone steps and push through the double doors. By the time we reach the auditorium, the room is abuzz—literally.

I duck just as a kid with dragon wings flies over me, nearly taking my head off. The place is packed and the volume level is deafening. Aside from the winged troublemakers divebombing their unsuspecting classmates, the rest of the kids are sitting with their sections. Through the crowd, I see the Juggernauts, the Freaks, and the Howlers, but I don't see our section.

"Over there," Rage says, pointing to the far side.

That's when I see a furry arm waving at us.

"There's Hairball," Rage says. "Let's go."

Well, here goes nothing.

I follow Rage through the crowd, and as I approach the Monstrosities I get a mixed reaction. Hairball and Stanphibian nod, but Aura crosses her arms and turns the other way. Wonderful.

I ignore her and take the empty seat beside her.

"Hey!" InvisiBill yells. "Get off of me!"

"Sorry," I say, moving over one.

As I settle in, I look up at the stage where the faculty is sitting. Professor Holmwood and Professor Morris are having an intense conversation, Professor Seward is flipping through a notebook, and Professor Hexum is staring straight ahead with his arms crossed and his walking stick across his lap.

As I look at him my blood boils, so I shift my attention to the large, black banner hanging above the stage. My eyes trace the bold, gothic letters that spell out the words: VAN HELSING ACADEMY. Then, I read the school's motto:

YOU MUST BELIEVE IN THINGS YOU
CANNOT IMAGINE.

When I first arrived, I had no idea what that meant. But now, after everything I've been through, I totally understand it. The things I've discovered here still boggle my mind. I mean, before this I had no idea that monsters were real.

Or that I'm a vampire.

Suddenly, I get knocked in the ribs.

"Hey!" I say, rubbing my side. But when I look to my left there's no one sitting there.

"Stop daydreaming," InvisiBill says. "Van Helsing is getting on stage."

I want to sock InvisiBill, but when I look up, Van Helsing is walking up the stairs with a strange man in tow. As usual, Van Helsing looks like he's dressed for a winter storm, complete with a sweater, gloves, and a scarf.

But I don't recognize the man behind him.

He's wearing a pair of thick, black glasses that seem odd against his pasty complexion. He has white hair like Van Helsing and is dressed in a black turtleneck shirt with brown pants. As Van Helsing approaches the microphone, he invites the man to stand beside him and the man complies, smiling nervously.

The microphone SQUEALS as Van Helsing pulls it towards him, making everyone cover their ears.

Then, the room grows quiet.

"Students," Van Helsing says, looking up. "We will begin once you ground yourselves and take your seats."

Seconds later, all of the flyers have touched down.

"Thank you," he says. "I have called this assembly to introduce an old friend who will be temporarily joining our faculty. It is my privilege to introduce Dr. Eugene Renfield."

As Van Helsing turns to Dr. Renfield, the other professors applaud, except for Hexum whose arms are still crossed. Dr. Renfield nods in acknowledgment but looks like he'd rather be anywhere else.

"Dr. Renfield will add much-needed expertise to our staff," Van Helsing continues. "He is the preeminent expert in the field of monster psychology. Dr. Renfield has conducted extensive field studies across all categories of monsters, publishing papers on nearly every monster sub-type. His knowledge of monster behavior and monster motivations are unparalleled and he will be a tremendous asset in helping us to better understand our opponents and ourselves. I am beyond thrilled that he has agreed to join us this term and starting tomorrow all of you will begin a new class called Monster Mindset 101."

"Wait, what?" Hairball blurts out, a little too loudly.

Van Helsing raises an eyebrow, but Hairball merely expressed what everyone else was thinking, because suddenly the room erupts in a collective groan.

And I can see why. I mean, how can we possibly take on a fifth class? We're buried up to our eyeballs in homework from the classes we already have.

"Well, this is a disaster," InvisiBill whispers. "I'm

barely passing as it is."

"Do not dismay," Van Helsing says. "I understand this is an additional course of study, but it is not my intention to overload you. What Dr. Renfield will teach you is invaluable. Therefore, there will be no homework assigned in his class. However, you must be an active participant to get a passing grade."

"Yep," InvisiBill whispers, "I'm definitely flunking that one too."

This time there's a collective cheer as the kids high-five or high-paw one another. Well, that's certainly a relief. I don't think I could handle one more thing.

"You will find your adjusted course schedules in your mailboxes," Van Helsing continues. "I know you all will make Dr. Renfield feel at home here. Thank you for attending this brief announcement. You are dismissed."

Suddenly, the room is buzzing once more as the kids stand up to leave. But I have a different idea. This might be my only chance to catch Van Helsing and get my team reinstated for the Monster Cup.

But as I head towards the stage I freeze.

For some reason, Dr. Renfield is looking my way.

For a second, I'm confused, and I look over my shoulder to see if he's staring at someone standing behind me, but there's no one there. And when I look back, he's still staring at me.

Then, Hexum puts his hand on Dr. Renfield's shoulder and he turns. Well, that was weird.

Now Van Helsing is talking to both Dr. Renfield and Hexum. Do I really want to bring this up with Hexum standing right there?

Probably not a good idea.

"Let's go check our mailboxes," Aura says. "I'm curious to see if we're having Monster Mindset in the morning or afternoon."

Suddenly, I hear snickering, and when I turn I see Harpoon pointing at me and whispering to the other Howlers. Then, they all burst out laughing.

"Shut up!" Aura yells. "You won on a technicality. Next year you won't be so lucky."

"Why's that?" Harpoon asks. "Are you getting rid of the vampire kid before next year's Monster Cup?"

The Howlers bend over in laughter.

"Come on, guys," Aura says, floating past them.

As we follow her out, I can tell she's still seething, but there's nothing I can do. At least she stuck up for me.

I guess that's a good thing.

But as soon as we step outside, we're stopped by our very own half-man, half-spider.

"Hang on, Monstrosities," Crawler says, blocking us with two of his spider legs. "I've been waiting for you."

"For us?" Aura says. "Why? We didn't do anything wrong. We were just heading back to Monster House."

"Relax," Crawler says. "You're not in trouble. I need your help. For a little job off campus."

"Off campus?" Rage says. "Whoa, hold on there.

Two

The last time we went off campus we got in really big trouble, remember? Like, we wrecked your jeep and nearly got eaten by zombies. Are you sure you're not looking for the Howlers?"

"Nope," Crawler says. "I'm looking for you guys."

"For what?" I ask. "And won't Van Helsing be mad at us for leaving school again?"

"Nope," Crawler says. "I'm following Van Helsing's orders."

"Really?" I say. "His orders for what?"

"For a mission," Crawler says.

"A mission, huh?" Hairball says, cracking his knuckles. "What kind of a mission?"

"Let's call it a search mission," Crawler says. "Follow me."

VAN HELSING ACADEMY

STUDENT ASSESSMENT

VITALS:
NAME: Bobby Rotunda
EYES: Brown
HAIR: None
HEIGHT: Unknown
WEIGHT: 1,000 lbs*
* Estimate

NOTES: A boneless, shapeless pile of flesh who can contort and stretch his body in an endless variety of ways. Has a voracious appetite.

CODENAME: Blobby

CLASSIFICATION TYPE:
Abnormal—Physical

SUPERNATURAL ASSESSMENT:

STRENGTH	●	●	●	●	○
AGILITY	●	○	○	○	○
FIGHTING	●	●	●	○	○
INTELLECT	●	○	○	○	○
CONTROL	●	●	●	○	○

TEACHABLE?	Yes	No
VAN HELSING	●	○
CRAWLER	●	○
HOLMWOOD	●	○
SEWARD	●	○
MORRIS	●	○
HEXUM	○	●
~~FAUSTIUS~~	~~○~~	~~○~~

RISK LEVEL: MEDIUM

CHAPTER THREE

GET ME OUT OF HERE

My gut is telling me this is a really, really bad idea.

After everything that's happened, the last thing I want to do is go on this little adventure. In fact, if I had it my way, I'd be back at Monster House lying in bed. But when Crawler 'volun-told' us that we were going with him on a "search mission"—whatever that means—everyone else jumped at the chance. So, I was forced to come along, whether I wanted to or not.

Of course, I could have backed out, but that would have irked the team even more. Right now, after blowing the team's shot at the Monster Cup, I need to do whatever it takes to mend fences. Especially with Aura, who still clearly hates me right now.

Like, really hates me right now.

She made that pretty obvious when we boarded the bus. I got on first and sat in the front. But Aura just floated past the empty seat next to me and went all the way to the back.

Message received.

Unfortunately, Stanphibian squeezed in next to me, so things are smelling rather fishy up here.

When it rains it pours.

Anyway, aside from my ghost-drama nobody even knows where the heck we're going because Crawler won't tell us. We've probably been on the road for half an hour and every time one of us asks if we're there yet, he just shakes his head and says, 'I'll tell you when we get there.'

I stare out the window at the passing trees when I suddenly remember something Crawler said when he roped us into this mission.

"Hey, Crawler," I say. "When you got us, you said you were following Van Helsing's orders. What exactly were his orders anyway?"

"He wants you guys to get more comfortable working together outside of the academy," Crawler says. "Let's just say your last two outings weren't exactly confidence builders."

Well, he's got that right.

The first time we left campus, we tried to stop a grave robbery and nearly got eaten by zombies and werewolves. That was totally scary, but it was relatively tame compared to my second time off campus.

That's when I got 'ported' through Professor Faustius' book into his secret lair and watched as he used my blood to bring Count Dracula back to life.

As much as I try, it's impossible to shake the fact that I've put the entire world in serious danger. I mean, no one talks about it around me, but I know everyone is nervous about how we'll stop Count Dracula—especially since Van Helsing said the only one who can actually do it is me.

Definitely not a confidence builder.

I mean, I know Count Dracula is out there somewhere gathering his strength. And now that he's back, I bet the Dark Ones' ranks are swelling right now. Apparently, evil is a magnet for demented people.

I look back out the window.

Then, I remember something else Crawler said and I shudder. It was right after he saved me from being demolished by Rage at the cemetery.

"Um, Crawler?" I call out. "Didn't you tell me we weren't safe once we left campus?"

"What, are you chicken now?" InvisiBill says from the seat behind me that I thought was empty. "We should call you Bawk-pire! Bawk, bawk!"

"I'm not a chicken, you goober," I say. "But after Crawler shot Rage with enough tranquilizers to put down a brontosaurus, he told me we weren't safe once we left the gates of the Van Helsing Academy. He said the school grounds are protected from evil by Supernatural artifacts, but we don't have that same protection once we leave campus. Isn't that right, Crawler?"

I catch Crawler looking at me wide-eyed in the rearview mirror. And when I turn around, the other kids are staring at me like I have two heads.

"Right, Crawler?" I say.

"Um, did I tell you that?" Crawler says.

"Yes," I say. "You did."

"Well, what do you know?" Crawler says, his voice rising. "I totally forgot about that."

"Great," Rage says, dropping his head into his hands. "Can we please turn around now?"

"But don't worry," Crawler says quickly. "This mission will be an easy one. And this time you're all under my supervision so it's cool. Hey, does anybody know some good road trip songs?"

"Hang on, Crawler," Aura says. "We're not just going to skip over this. How come no one told us the school has Supernatural protection?"

"Never came up?" Crawler offers.

"Spill it, Crawler," Hairball says. "What are these artifacts already?"

"Nothing, really," he says. "Oh my, look at that tree over there. Is that a squirrel?"

"Stop trying to change the subject," InvisiBill says.

"It's a big squirrel," Crawler says. "Look at its—"

"Spill it!" we all yell in unison.

"Okay, okay," Crawler says. "But I'm not supposed to talk about this. If I tell you, you can't repeat it to anyone—and I mean anyone. Do we have a deal?"

"Deal," we all agree.

"Alright," Crawler says, his eyes narrowing. "Legend has it that somewhere, hidden in the basement of the Van

Helsing Academy are three Supernatural objects—a bell, a book, and a candle—known as the Artifacts of Virtue. Now I've never seen them myself, but it's said that as long as they're aligned to form a triangle, they cast a shield of protection that blocks evil from breaking through their barrier."

"Hold on," InvisiBill says. "Are you saying the entire school is protected by a bell, a book, and a dinky candle?"

"Yep," Crawler says. "That's what I'm saying."

"Is it really true?" Aura asks.

"Ever seen any zombies in Monster House or werewolves on the quad?" Crawler says.

"Well, no," I say.

"I guess you have your answer then," Crawler says. "Now look alive because we're finally here. Thank goodness."

Here? Here where?

Out the window I see a battered blue sign:

MOREAU LABORATORIES

Moreau Laboratories? What's that?

But as I look up, I'm not sure I want to know the answer, because standing before us is a creepy office building that's seen way better days. It's three stories tall with a cracked brick facade and boarded-up windows. The overgrown bushes clearly haven't been trimmed in years and the chain-link fence surrounding the perimeter looks like it was run over by a tank.

"Were not going in there, are we?" Rage asks.

"Yes, we are," Crawler says.

"But it looks like the set of a horror movie," Rage says. "Like, a really scary horror movie."

"Well," Crawler says. "I guess it's a good thing we're monsters."

As we head down the driveway, I realize there aren't any streetlights. And as we get closer to the building, I notice empty guard towers and rolls of barbed wire stretched across the ground. Clearly, this was once a heavily fortified complex. But the question is why?

Crawler pulls into the parking lot and parks in the faded handicapped space right in front of the building. Normally, I'd tell him that's rude, but since it doesn't seem like anyone has parked here for decades, we're probably okay.

"Everyone out," Crawler says.

As we file out, it dawns on me that we can forget about the element of surprise. I mean, it's not like Crawler is trying to hide us.

"Okay," Crawler says, slapping two of his spider legs together. "Here's the deal. As you know, my spider network has eyes all over the world. Yesterday, one of my top scouts spotted strange activity here at Moreau Labs. For those of you who don't know what Moreau Labs is—which is pretty much all of you by the looks of it—let me give you a quick rundown. Moreau Labs was a

government-backed research facility run by a man named
Dr. Simon Moreau, a brilliant but misguided scientist who
became infamous for conducting genetic experiments on
regular people… and, well, monsters."

"Monsters?" Rage says. "Did you just say monsters?"

"Um, what kinds of experiments?" InvisiBill asks.

"Not good ones," Crawler says. "But don't worry,
his lab has been shut down for a long, long time. The
government didn't agree with whatever Moreau was
doing, so they pulled his funding and came to arrest him.
But Moreau escaped, went into hiding, and hasn't been
seen since. His lab has been vacant for years. Until now,
that is."

"Well, this just keeps getting better," I say. "What
exactly does 'until now' mean?"

"It means my scout picked up movement inside the
lab," Crawler says. "But it's nothing to be nervous about.
According to her final report, the lab has been infiltrated
by a couple of cats."

"Cats?" I say. "Like, kitty cats?"

"Exactly," Crawler says.

"So," I say. "what's the problem if cats are running
around this old building?"

"Because we've been keeping our eyes on this facility
ever since Dr. Moreau got away," Crawler says. "And this
is the first activity we've picked up since he left. We just
need to make sure everything checks out okay, that's all."

"Just one more question," Aura asks. "You said your

scout made her final report. What does 'final' mean?"

"It means I haven't heard from her since," Crawler says, his eyebrows rising with concern. "And she's not responding to any communication."

"Well, that's reassuring," I say. "Anything else you're not telling us?"

"Nope," Crawler says. "So, let's break up into smaller groups and sweep this building fast."

***

Well, so much for being under Crawler's direct supervision. Crawler split us into teams and we went our separate ways. Aura and Hairball got the first floor, Crawler, InvisiBill, and Stanphibian took the second floor, and Rage and I got the top floor. Not that I'm complaining. Believe me, I want to get this over with as quickly as possible.

The good news is that Crawler is keeping close tabs on InvisiBill and Stanphibian. If those two knuckleheads were left to their own devices, they'd definitely screw something up big time.

As Rage and I climb the last flight of stairs I notice him falling behind. I glance over my shoulder and see he's wincing, holding his head with one hand, and gripping the railing tight with the other.

"You okay?" I whisper.

"What?" Rage says, standing up straighter. "Yeah,

sorry. It's just… I'm fine."

Okay, I don't know what's wrong with him, but that's even more incentive to get this done fast. As I step onto the third-floor landing. I listen for the telltale sounds of cats, like purring, meowing, or the yakking of a hairball, but there's nothing. I guess this is where the 'search' part of the search mission comes in.

I peer around the corner of the stairwell down a long hallway. The square, overhead lights are out, the beige floor tiles run from end-to-end, and all of the doors along the hallway are closed.

Then, I notice something strange.

At the far end of the hallway is a smashed window with glass shards and a shattered wood panel scattered on the floor. Clearly, something busted its way inside. My first thought is the cats, but I don't think cats could climb three stories up the side of a building and smash through a boarded-up window.

"Here, kitty kitty," I call out.

"Shhh!" Rage whispers, coming up behind me. "What do you think you're doing?"

"Trying to find some cats," I say. "Do you want to be here all night?"

"Well, no," he says. "But I…"

The next thing I know, Rage wobbles, and I grab his arm, keeping him from falling over.

"Whoa," I say. "You okay?"

"Yeah," he says. "Just a little disoriented for some

reason."

"Okay," I say. "Lean against the wall here while I open these doors one by one. If any cats are up here, they'll probably be in one of these rooms."

I try every door, but they're all locked. And each one features a different plaque describing what's inside, like *Medical Supplies*, *Sanitation Chamber*, and *Disposal Room*.

We're halfway down the hall when I notice something else. Beneath the farthest door on the right is a faint sliver of light. Is someone in there?

I'm about to tell Rage when he suddenly says—

"I-I think I've been here before."

"What?" I say. But when I turn around, Rage is sliding down the wall, his eyes darting all over.

"I-I know this place," Rage says, breathing faster like he's hyperventilating.

"Hey, relax," I say. "Are you o—"

But before I can finish my sentence, his eyes roll back in his head and he crumples to the ground, hitting his head on a doorknob on the way down.

"Rage!" I yell, running over to him.

By the time I reach him he's out for the count. Fortunately, he's still breathing. I slap his face lightly to rouse him, but he won't wake up.

"Come on, Rage," I say, turning his head gently.

Then, I freeze.

There, on his left temple, is a thin trickle of blood.

It's not a lot, but it's dripping down the side of his

face. Suddenly, my stomach rumbles, and I remember I haven't eaten dinner. I lick my lips.

Boy, that red liquid sure looks good.

Wait, what?

I shake my head. I mean, what's happening? Where did that come from?

I… I don't drink blood.

Never.

I try putting it out of my mind and focus back on Rage. I don't know what happened to him but we can forget looking for these crazy cats. Rage needs help.

I've got to get him out of here, but how? He probably doesn't weigh a ton. So, should I try carrying him downstairs on my own or should I leave him here and go get the others?

Just then, I hear footsteps coming from behind me.

I breathe a sigh of relief.

"Crawler!" I say. "Thank goodness, Rage just passed out so maybe you can—"

But when I look up my heart stops.

Because I'm not staring at Crawler.

But rather a pair of red, luminous eyes.

CHAPTER FOUR

CAT FIGHT

I can't believe what I'm seeing.

Because standing over Rage and me, snarling in a low, rather unfriendly tone, is some kind of a half-boy, half-beast! His body looks completely normal, but his head is shaped like... a tiger?

My instincts tell me to run, but I can't just leave Rage lying here unconscious. I don't know who this tiger kid is or what he's doing here, but then it dawns on me. Could this be the cat Crawler's scout was referring to?

And if so, is he responsible for smashing through the boarded-up window at the end of the hallway? My eyes drift down to his sharp claws. Well, he certainly looks like he could climb up the side of a building.

Then, I realize something. We've been staring at each other for a good few seconds and he hasn't attacked us yet. Why hasn't he attacked us yet?

"Easy, fella," I say, rising slowly.

Tiger-boy growls and I freeze, my body stuck in a

crouched position. That's when I notice he doesn't seem much taller than I am. He's wearing jeans and a black t-shirt that says, "Rock On," and his arms are down by his sides which isn't exactly a threatening posture. In fact, I don't think he's planning on attacking us at all.

And then I hear him breathing. It sounds like he's wheezing—like he's struggling to catch his breath.

"Hey, it's okay," I say, putting my hands up. "I'm not here to fight you."

He tilts his head, his pointy ears pricking up.

I wonder if he understands me.

"My name is Bram," I say, pointing to my heart. "We just came here to find some cats. And, um, I'm thinking that might be you. Do you have a name?"

But when I point at him he jumps back to the window so fast it surprises me.

"It's okay," I say, reassuringly. "We're not here to hurt you." I look down at Rage who's still not stirring. "My friend needs help. Do you need help?"

Tiger-boy slowly moves in front of the last door on the right. That's the one with the light coming from beneath it. But then I notice the door is still closed. For a second I'm confused because I assumed he came through that door. But clearly, he didn't.

Suddenly, he turns the knob and pushes the door open. As it swings inward, more light pours into the hallway and I can see Tiger-boy even more clearly. For the first time, I notice he doesn't look so good. His orange fur is mangy and there are bald patches on one side of his head.

"Are you sick?" I ask. "If you come with me, I can help you. I have friends that can help you."

For a brief second, his eyes grow wide, like he wants to come with me more than anything, but then he nods towards the open doorway and growls. It's like he wants me to go in there. But before I can ask him what's inside, he rushes to the window with uncanny quickness and leaps outside!

"Wait!" I yell, running to the window.

But by the time I get there, he's long gone. I try spotting him in the underbrush but I can't. And all he's left behind is a shred of his t-shirt that's hanging off the windowpane. Man, he's powerful. I mean, we're three stories off the ground!

Ugh, now I'll never know who he is or what he was doing here. He looked like he was in some kind of serious trouble. Speaking of trouble, I've got to get back to Rage.

But as soon as I turn around, I hear moaning.

Rage is still out so that couldn't be him.

Am I hearing things?

Then, it comes again. It's a bit louder this time, and it's coming from inside the open room! I hesitate. Maybe I should call the others.

"Ohhh," comes a girl's voice.

This time I hear it clearly. Someone is definitely in there, and she sounds like she's hurt. There might not be time to get the others.

I approach the door cautiously and peer inside. The room looks like a patient recovery room, with a hospital bed and monitoring equipment. The first bed is empty, but there's a curtain drawn across the center of the room, blocking the second bed.

"Uhhhnnn," comes the voice again.

Okay, that came from behind the curtain!

I step inside softly, and as I get closer to the curtain I can see the shadow of someone lying on the bed.

I hold my breath, grab the curtain, and yank it back.

Then, I do a double take.

Because lying on the bed is a half-cat, half-girl!

***

"She's stable," Dr. Hagella says, "but barely. It's a good thing you found her when you did. She's malnourished and I'm not sure she would have survived another day in her state. I need to get more fluids. I'll be back in a few minutes."

As Dr. Hagella exits I breathe a sigh of relief. Cat-girl is resting comfortably in Dr. Hagella's infirmary, hooked up to monitors and an IV. Dr. Hagella cleaned her up a bit, and as I study her face it's interesting how different she looks from Tiger-boy.

While Tiger-boy was more like an animal than a human, Cat-girl is more human than animal. Yet, her cat features are clearly there. White, fuzzy ears protrude from her platinum-blond hair, and razor-thin whiskers extend beyond her cheeks. And it's hard not to notice her sharp fingernails, pointy teeth, and long, furry tail which is hanging off the bed.

Fortunately, Crawler and the others showed up right after I found her. And based on Crawler's reaction when he saw her, she wasn't the type of cat he was expecting to find either. On the ride back to Van Helsing Academy, I told the team about my encounter with Tiger-boy, but no one saw him but me.

I'm just glad we were able to get Cat-girl into Dr. Hagella's care when we did. Dr. Hagella is an expert in monster biology, and she seemed to know exactly what Cat-girl needed. Which is more than I can say for myself.

Honestly, this whole episode has left me more than a little freaked out. Our run-in with the cat-kids wasn't the only bizarre thing that happened. I mean, I nearly drank Rage's blood! I look over at poor Rage who is lying unconscious in the next bed.

Where did that crazy urge come from? I mean, I've never E-V-E-R had the desire to drink anyone's blood. I've been trying to put that near-disaster out of my mind, but I just can't shake it.

Maybe I should tell Van Helsing?

But if I do, what will he think of me? I mean, it only happened once. I'm sure it won't happen again. Right?

Well, it's a moot point for now anyway. As soon as

we brought Cat-girl back to school, Van Helsing took one look at her and informed us he had to leave immediately. I then overheard him whispering to Crawler about rounding up some of the other professors and heading back to Moreau Labs.

Then, they took off.

"Man," InvisiBill says from somewhere on the other side of the room. "I'm wiped. I'm gonna head back to Monster House for some shuteye. Anyone want to come?"

"I'm in," Hairball says, stretching into a big yawn. "There's nothing for us to do here. You coming, Aura?"

"No," she says. "I don't need sleep, remember? And besides, I want to stay until Rage wakes up."

"Suit yourself," Hairball says. "Night."

"I'm good," I say to no one in particular. "Thanks for asking."

As Hairball exits, Stanphibian waves a webbed hand and follows him out. I see a bunch of cords move on their own by the doorway which likely means InvisiBill is right behind them.

It's just Aura and me.

"Funny how we keep ending up together like this," I say.

But Aura doesn't respond. Instead, she crosses her arms and floats closer to check on Rage. Great, she's still mad at me. Talk about holding a grudge!

I'm about to apologize again for ruining the Monster

Cup when—

"Stop!" Rage yells, sitting up suddenly.

"Rage, relax," Aura says. "It's okay. You're back at school."

"What?" Rage says with panic in his eyes. "Where?"

"Back at school," Aura says. "At the Van Helsing Academy. You're home now. It's okay."

Rage looks around and then wipes his forehead which is covered in sweat.

"Are you okay?" I ask. "Do you remember anything before you passed out?"

"Y-Yeah," he says, looking confused. "We were at Moreau Labs, and suddenly everything came rushing back. I-I remembered… things."

Suddenly, the hairs on the back of my neck stand on end. When I first met Rage, he told me he had no memory of his past. In fact, he said his very first memory was waking up here at the Van Helsing Academy.

"What kinds of things?" Aura asks.

"I-I remember being wheeled down a hallway on a gurney," he says. "It was a long, narrow hallway just like the one we were in. And… and I remember the smell. It smelled… medical. Like… disinfectant. And…"

Rage opens his mouth but no words come out.

"And what?" Aura prods. "Come on, Rage. This could be important. You can do it."

"And then I remember being pushed into a room with a bright light overhead." Rage says. "Everything was kind of foggy but I could hear scraping. Like metal on metal. And the room was so cold I was shivering. And then, out of nowhere, I saw… him."

As Rage's voice trails off I can tell he's back there—back in that moment when his nightmare started.

"Who?" I say. "Who did you see?"

"A-A man," Rage says. "An older man, with white hair and… cold, gray eyes. And before he put his surgical mask on he smiled and said, 'Don't worry, this won't hurt—at least not too much.'"

Aura looks at me with sad eyes.

"I… I think that was him," Rage says.

"Who?" I ask.

"Moreau," Rage says. "I-I think Dr. Moreau did this to me. I think Dr. Moreau made me into a monster."

CHAPTER FIVE

TRANCE-SYLVANIA

Unfortunately, Van Helsing isn't back from Moreau Labs yet, so we have to sit tight on Rage's shocking news.

I feel bad for the kid. I mean, I can't even imagine the horrors he's reliving in his mind. And after he told us that he was one of Dr. Moreau's victims, another stress wave kicked in and he passed out again. Not that I can blame him.

And since Cat-girl hasn't woken up yet either, Dr. Hagella said there's no point in us just hanging around doing nothing. So, she sent us to class. Yippee. That's pretty much the last place I want to be right now.

Especially since it's our first day with super creepy Dr. Renfield.

"Welcome, students," Dr. Renfield says, standing at the front of the classroom with a pointer in his hand. "Please take out your notebooks. Today, I will be providing a comprehensive introduction to Monster Mindset 101, the fundamentals of monster psychology."

Great. Just what I need.

As I look around I realize I'm far from alone in my thinking. Stanphibian is doodling in his notebook, Hairball is half-asleep, and InvisiBill's chair appears empty because it probably is.

Then, there's Aura.

No surprise, she's sitting front and center at full attention. She loves learning new things, but even more impressively, she somehow retains it all. I bet she uses all of that time she's not sleeping to study.

Me? I could use a good snooze. Especially right now.

"Now," Dr. Renfield continues, "I am sure you are wondering what the exciting field of monster psychology is all about."

No, not really. But I am wondering if I'm going to survive this class. I mean, Dr. Renfield isn't the most dynamic teacher I've ever had. Hmmm, I wonder how long it would take me to count the ceiling tiles?

"As Headmaster Van Helsing explained," Dr. Renfield drones on. "It is frequently said that the human mind is one of nature's most astonishing creations. That may be true, but I can assure you that the mind of the monster is a wonder unlike anything produced in common nature. First, we will—"

"Pssst," comes a sharp whisper from behind.

I turn around to find Harpoon staring at me with her beady, yellow eyes. Then, she smirks and passes me a note. What could this be?

"I have psycho-analyzed every major classification of

monster," Dr. Renfield continues, completely oblivious to what's going on, "and nearly every sub-classification. I have dedicated my life to understanding the motivations of monsters. From shapeshifters to spirits. From the undead to the abnormal. Here, in this classroom, we will unlock the mysteries of the monster mind together. But this class will be more than lectures. It will also be quite hands-on. You see, most of my findings have been discovered through the science of hypnosis. Hypnosis is the—"

I tune Dr. Renfield out as I quietly unfold Harpoon's note under my desk. It reads:

> I DARE U TO PASS THIS NOTE.
> UNLESS U R A CHICKEN.

Seriously? And what's with the chicken thing?

I look back at Harpoon who mouths chicken noises. This is ridiculous. I'm not going to pass a note in the middle of class. I crumple it up.

"Pssst," comes another whisper, this time from over my left shoulder.

I turn to find Gnatalie and MinoTodd mouthing the same chicken noises. Okay, the last thing I need is for all of the Howlers to think I'm a chicken too. Especially after losing to them in the Monster Cup.

If passing this note will get them off my back, then I'll just pass the darn note.

But to who?

Hairball is closest, but he looks like he's sleeping. If I give it to him, I'll just have to be sure he won't make a scene. I wait for Dr. Renfield to write on the blackboard, and then whisper sharply—

"Hairball."

"Wha—?" he says, jolting upright, his big hairy arm slipping from his chin and banging on his desktop.

Oh jeez!

But thankfully, Dr. Renfield doesn't notice.

"Take this," I whisper, handing over the note.

But before Hairball can grab it—BOOM—it explodes into a ball of black smoke!

What happened?

"Who did that?" Dr. Renfield says, looking my way.

But when I turn around, all I see are the Howlers laughing to themselves, including Lucky and his cursed amulet. Suddenly, it all makes sense.

They set me up.

That note was cursed the whole time.

I'm such an idiot.

"You there," Dr. Renfield says, pointing at me. "Come to the front of the class."

Great. Here we go.

As I stand up, I debate whether I should tattle on the Howlers or not, but then decide against it. After all, what good would it do? I passed the note, so I'll just have to take my punishment like a man.

"Stand here," Dr. Renfield says, pointing to a spot in front of the whole class.

I dutifully take my mark and stand quietly, my hands fidgeting behind my back. I try to appear calm but my imagination is spinning. Why did he pull me up here? Why didn't he just send me to Van Helsing's office? At least I could set my own punishment then.

"You are Mr. Murray," Dr. Renfield says. "Is that correct?"

"Um, yeah," I say, surprised that he even knows my name. I mean, he didn't even take roll call when the class started. But then I remember him staring at me after the assembly.

"I thought so," Dr. Renfield says. "Mr. Murray, you will be our first volunteer."

"Um, volunteer for what?" I ask.

"For hypnosis, of course," Dr. Renfield says, as he reaches into his coat pocket and pulls out a gold pendulum. It's circular and hanging from a gold chain. "If you were listening, you would have learned that this is my primary method for uncovering the motivations of monsters."

"And what exactly does that mean?" I ask.

"There is nothing to fear," Dr. Renfield says. "Hypnosis is simply a technique that will put you in a very relaxed state of mind—a trance if you will—allowing you to reach a heightened state of awareness. How does that sound?"

"Weird," I answer, as the class laughs.

"Now, as I understand it, Mr. Murray, you are a vampire, a rare sub-species not seen for quite a long time. In fact, as far as I am aware, no psychologist has ever hypnotized a vampire before. This will be a first in the field of monster psychology."

"Um, okay," I say, not sure how to respond. But he seems rather excited.

"Now," Dr. Renfield says, swinging the pendulum in front of my face. "Try to relax as we begin."

"Um, hang on a sec," I say, swallowing hard. "Is this really a good idea?"

"I think it is an excellent idea," Dr. Renfield says. "Unless, of course, you are afraid?"

The class giggles again, and I look out at all of the faces staring at me. That's when Harpoon mouths more chicken noises.

"N-No," I say. "I'm not afraid. I'm good."

"I thought you would be," Dr. Renfield says. "After all, vampires are notorious for their courage. Now, I want you to relax and stare at the pendulum."

My eyes follow the gold pendulum as it swings back and forth from his fingers in a slow, regular rhythm. I don't know what he's getting at but I might as well play along. I'm sure this hypnotism thing only works in the movies.

"Notice how the pendulum moves as you breathe slowly," Dr. Renfield says. "And as you continue to watch, you may notice your eyelids becoming heavy as you start to relax."

Hmm, that's funny. My eyelids are getting heavier. In fact, I'm having a hard time keeping them open.

"You may notice as you continue to breathe you have the urge to blink," Dr. Renfield says. "That is completely normal. But, if you are ready, go ahead and close your eyes fully."

As my lids press down, I realize that even if I wanted to open my eyes, I couldn't.

In fact, I can't move a muscle.

"And as you continue to relax and breathe," Dr. Renfield says soothingly, "we shall begin…"

***

"… now wide awake," comes a voice.

SNAP!

My eyes pop open and I'm disoriented.

Where am I?

Then, as my vision readjusts, I realize I'm standing in front of the entire class! And they're all staring at me with big, goofy smiles on their faces. Suddenly, I feel my face go flush—or, at least as flush as it can go given my pale complexion.

What's going on? Why are they looking at me?

"How do you feel?" comes a voice to my right, surprising me.

I turn to find Dr. Renfield standing next to me. In his hand is that gold pendulum. Then, it dawns on me. He just hypnotized me!

"How do you feel, Mr. Murray?" Dr. Renfield repeats.

"Um, okay," I lie, crossing my arms. Truthfully, I feel kind of exposed right now. I mean, I don't remember anything that just happened.

Just then, the bell RINGS.

Class is over.

All of the students jump up in unison and begin to file past me and out the door.

"Well, that was… interesting," Hairball says, giving me a wink.

"You've got some pretty serious issues," I hear InvisiBill say. "You may want to see somebody about that."

"Wow," is all Stanphibian offers.

Now, panic sets in. I mean, what just happened?

What did he ask me?

What did I say?

Then, I see Aura with her eyebrows raised. Uh-oh.

"Were you really hypnotized?" she asks. "You weren't pretending, were you?"

"No," I say, exhaling. "Why, how bad was it?"

"Not too bad," she says. "Don't listen to those idiots. They're just messing with you. Dr. Renfield only asked you simple questions. Like, what's your favorite food, and what's your greatest fear."

"Wait, he asked me that?" I say, more panic setting in. I can't imagine how I answered that one. Hopefully, I didn't say clowns. Boy, do I hate clowns. Okay, I need to stay calm. "Um, so, what did I say?"

"Count Dracula," she says. "But don't worry. Pretty much everyone knew that already. I think it's pretty obvious given present circumstances."

"Yeah," I say, a little freaked out that I told everyone my greatest fear is the one person I'm destined to destroy.

"I wouldn't worry about it," she says. "Dr. Renfield was just demonstrating how the power of hypnosis can dig deep into the monster mind. It was actually interesting. You just went along with whatever he asked you to do. Who knew that hypnosis was such a powerful tool?"

"Well, isn't that just wonderful," I say, rubbing my head. "But I think I'm done volunteering for a while. I'm really not the Guinea pig-type. I'm just glad I didn't make too much of a fool of myself. Right?"

"Nope," she says. "You've pretty much done that already. See you later."

Then, she smiles and phases through the wall.

Right.

I'm the last kid in the room, so I go back to my desk to grab my stuff when I hear—

"How are you feeling, Mr. Murray?"

I freeze. It's Dr. Renfield.

"Oh, great," I say, lying through my teeth. "I'm fine. Well, I don't want to be late for my next class, so…"

"If you would allow me just one more moment, Mr. Murray," Dr. Renfield says, approaching me.

"Um, okay," I say reluctantly.

He stops in front of me and smiles.

"As I mentioned earlier," he says, "No psychologist has ever had the pleasure of delving into the mind of a vampire before. But it seems that fate has shined on both of us, because here we are, together at the famed Van Helsing Academy. Me, the world's leading monster psychologist, and you, one of the world's last remaining vampires. Wouldn't you agree that this is the opportunity of a lifetime?"

"Well, no," I say. "Not really."

"Together," he continues, "we can make scientific history. With just a few more sessions, we could easily reveal the inner workings of the vampire mind. Imagine the groundbreaking papers we could publish. Imagine the accolades we would receive."

"Wait," I say. "Are you asking to hypnotize me again? Like, a lot of times?"

"Oh, yes," he says. "I imagine the experience was painless for you, wasn't it? We would only need a few more sessions to do this properly. Of course, I would compile all of the findings and write all of the papers. You just need to show up."

Okay, this guy is nuts.

I'm not getting hypnotized again. Like, never again in my entire life. I've got to get out of here.

"Oh, that sounds like a generous offer," I say. "But I have to be honest. I'm really not interested. You see, I've got all of these other commitments, like class, and homework, and trying not to make a fool of myself everywhere I go. So, I've got to run along now."

"Are you sure?" he asks.

"Yeah," I say. "I'm sure. Rock-solid sure."

"Oh," he says, disappointed. "Of course. Perhaps we can revisit this topic at another time."

"Great," I say, moving around him for the door.

"Oh, one more thing Mr. Murray," Dr. Renfield says.

"Yeah?" I say, turning in the doorframe.

"You may experience some… lingering dizziness from the hypnosis," he says. "But don't worry, it's completely normal and you'll be just fine."

"Oh, okay," I say. "Thanks for letting me know."

Then, I take off as fast as I can.

CLASSIFIED

Person(s) of Interest

CODE NAME: NONE

REAL NAME: DR. EUGENE RENFIELD

BASE OF OPERATIONS: VAN HELSING ACADEMY

Category: Natural

Sub-Type: Not Applicable

Height: 5'10"

Weight: 195 lbs

FACTS: Dr. Renfield is the preeminent expert in the field of monster psychology. Dr. Renfield has studied nearly every sub-type of monster and publishes his findings in scientific journals. He is currently working as an adjunct professor at the Van Helsing Academy.

FIELD OBSERVATIONS:

- Expert in the science of hypnosis
- Highly intelligent
- Frequently travels for field research
- A former schoolmate of Lothar Van Helsing

STATUS: ACTIVE TARGET

DEPARTMENT OF SUPERNATURAL INVESTIGATIONS

CHAPTER SIX

FEVER DREAMS

We got quite a surprise before lights out.

There I was, brushing my teeth and thinking about my super-strange encounter with Dr. Renfield when Hairball barges through the bathroom door.

"Come downstairs," he says. "Van Helsing is back and wants to see us in the foyer."

I rinse quickly and spit. Van Helsing is back? And he's here in the Monster House foyer? I don't think I've ever seen Van Helsing in Monster House before. And since he was just out visiting Moreau Labs, he must be here on serious business.

For a split second, I debate getting dressed but given the seriousness of the situation, I prioritize speed over style and go downstairs in my pajamas.

When I reach the bottom, I find I'm not the only one. Hairball and Stanphibian are in their pj's too, while who knows what InvisiBill is wearing. Of course, Aura is a ghost, so she's always dressed the same.

And, just as Hairball promised, Van Helsing is here

waiting for us, but he's not alone. Crawler, Professor Morris, and Rage are with him too.

Boy, it's great seeing Rage on his feet again, and he's wearing a small bandage on his head where he got injured. He smiles when he sees me but based on the gloomy expressions on the adults' faces, it's clear they're not here for a celebration.

"Thank you all for joining us at this late hour," Van Helsing says. "Based on your trip to Moreau Labs, your discovery of the 'Cat-girl,' as you call her, and your concern for the wellbeing of your colleague, Rage, who has made a full recovery, I thought it would be best to update you all on what we have discovered."

"About time," InvisiBill says.

"As you know, I returned to Moreau Labs with Crawler and Professor Morris to examine the site," Van Helsing says. "The evidence we recovered is conclusive. Dr. Moreau is back in operation."

As soon as Van Helsing finishes his sentence, a chill runs down my spine.

"I'm guessing that's a bad thing," InvisiBill says.

"Yes," Van Helsing says. "Very bad. You see, before he was pursued by the government, Dr. Moreau conducted horrific experiments, bending the laws of nature for his own devious purposes. In particular, he was known for transforming innocent people into terrors known as 'Hybrids.'"

"Hybrids?" Aura says. "What's that?"

"A Hybrid is a term used to describe the combination of a human with an animal," Van Helsing says. "For example, a Goat-man or a—"

"—Cat-girl?" I say, finishing his sentence.

"Yes," Van Helsing says. "Dr. Moreau created many of these Hybrid creatures. He claimed that he was doing it for the good of all—that he was creating a new species of mankind that could serve humanity—but his experiments never survived for long. When Dr. Moreau went underground, we thought we were finally free of his evil ways. But sadly, he has returned."

I swallow hard.

My thoughts go back to Tiger-boy and Cat-girl. Based on what Van Helsing is saying, who knows how long they'll live? Tiger-boy looked sick, and Cat-girl is in pretty bad shape. Maybe she won't make it.

"I scanned the entire building with my DNA probe," Professor Morris says, holding up a silver device that looks like an eggbeater. "There was no evidence of Moreau anywhere, except for this."

As Professor Morris pulls out a piece of black cloth, my eyes go wide.

"The Tiger-boy was wearing that," I say. "It tore off his body when he jumped out the window."

"Well, guess what," Professor Morris says. "It's got Dr. Moreau's fingerprints on it. A perfect match."

"Wow," I say. "What about Cat-girl?"

"Glad to see you're thinking like a Supernatural

crime scene investigator," Professor Morris says. "Yes, she has the same prints on her clothing."

"Let's go talk to her," Aura says. "She has to know something."

"Unfortunately, she is still unconscious," Van Helsing says. "We will speak with her when she comes to, but we must do so delicately as she will likely be in a state of shock. I know I have provided you with a lot of information, but I ask that you keep it confidential. Tonight, your only job is to take care of your friend, Rage. He has recovered well, but he'll surely need your support."

"You can count on us," I say. "He's in good hands."

"I thought so," Van Helsing says. "Now, good night, Monstrosities. Sleep well."

"You too," Aura says.

Van Helsing nods at me and then exits, followed by Crawler and Professor Morris.

"Are you okay?" I ask Rage, putting my hand on his shoulder.

"Yeah," he says. "I don't know what happened. I was just overwhelmed being back in that building. It was just weird. What do they call it when it feels like you're reliving something you've experienced before?"

"Doggie-doo," InvisiBill says.

"No, you moron," Aura says. "It's called déjà vu."

"Oh, right," InvisiBill says. "Just kidding."

"Anyway," I say. "It's late. Maybe we should go

upstairs and finish getting ready for bed."

"Yeah, I'm pretty tired," Rage says, touching his bandage.

Suddenly, I feel an overwhelming sense of guilt. I mean, I nearly drank the poor guy's blood. What kind of a teammate am I?

"Let's head up," I say. "I'll help you pull your stuff together so you can go right to sleep."

"Thanks," Rage says, putting his arm around me. "You know, Bram, I'm lucky to have you as a friend."

***

I'm walking down a long, narrow hallway—except, it's not a hallway at all—it's a tunnel. The air is cold and musty, and as I walk, my arms brush against the rocky walls. Unlit torches hang from the wall every ten feet or so, but I don't need them to see. Strangely, a dribbling sound echoes through the tunnel, like running water, but I don't see a water source anywhere.

Occasionally, I need to stoop beneath the low, uneven ceiling to continue, and I suddenly feel claustrophobic, like the tunnel is closing in on me.

On the inside, I feel a burning desire to turn around, but my feet keep moving forward, step by step along the craggy floor. My entire body feels… odd. It's like I'm not in control of my movements.

I try calling for help. For Rage, or Aura, or Van

Helsing, but my lips won't form the words.

Then, the tunnel bends.

I follow it around, not that I have a choice. I'm like a passenger in an out-of-control car, but that car happens to be my own body.

Then, I see it.

The end of the tunnel, about twenty yards ahead.

And flush against the rock wall is an iron vault door.

Immediately, my alarm bells go off. There's something strange about this door. I mean, I don't know of any vault doors attached to rock walls. On the door itself is a small wheel that must be the locking mechanism. If I turn the wheel, the door will swing wide open.

I have an overwhelming desire to head back, but I can't. Instead, I walk over and stop in front of the door.

Suddenly, I notice it's deathly quiet. I don't hear the sound of water anymore. All I hear is the pounding of my own heart.

Then, there's a FLAPPING noise.

I don't see anything flying around me. In fact, if I didn't know better, I'd say that noise sounded like it came from the other side of the—

"Will you open the door?" a male voice asks.

I jump. Who was that?

"Will you open the door?" he repeats.

Okay, that definitely came from the other side of the door. And even though his voice sounded friendly, I feel like I've heard that deep, raspy tone before.

"Who are you?" I say, finding my voice again.

"A friend," he says. *"Will you please open the door?"*

"No," I say.

"Very well," he says. *"Then I will have to do it myself."*

Suddenly, my arms start moving towards the wheel.

No!

I focus everything I have on stopping myself, but my arms just won't listen.

What's happening?

"That's it," he says, his voice rising with excitement. *"Just turn the wheel. Trust me, you won't regret it."*

No! I… won't turn it! But despite my protests, my hands grip the cold, rusty wheel.

"Very good, Bram," he says. *"Now just turn it."*

I try screaming 'NO,' but instead, I feel the corners of my mouth expanding upwards, getting itself ready to say the word 'YES!'

NO!

NO!

N—

***

—O!"

"Bram?"

My eyes pop open, and I'm no longer standing in a tunnel, but rather sitting up in my bed. My skin feels clammy and I'm covered in sweat. How did I get here?

I lift my arms. They're back in my control.

"Bram?" comes Rage's voice.

Rage is standing next to me in his pajamas. What's he doing out of bed? I mean, the last thing I remember was helping him get into his bed. Then, I waited for him to fall asleep before I left the room to go for a walk.

So, what am I doing in my bed?

With my shoes on?

"Bram?" Rage says again. "Are you okay? You look kind of freaked out. It sounded like you had a bad dream or something?"

Was it a dream?

I guess it could have been. But everything felt so… real? And who was behind that door? Who wanted me to open the door so badly? And more importantly, why?

"Um, yeah," I say, trying to act natural. For some reason, I feel like I shouldn't tell him about it. I'll just tell him about one of my other dreams. "It's nothing. Now and then I have this weird nightmare where I'm a bat being chased by baseballs. Don't ask. Anyway, what are you doing up? I thought you were sound asleep?"

"I was," he says. "But InvisiBill woke me up."

"InvisiBill?" I say, looking around, not like I could see him even if he was here. "What for? What time is it?"

"After midnight," Rage says. "InvisiBill said we need to meet in the common room. He said the Howlers are waiting for us. He said they gave us a dare."

"A dare?" I ask. "What kind of a dare?"

"Well," Rage says. "Apparently, InvisiBill spilled the beans about the Artifacts of Virtue."

"WHAT?" I exclaim. "Crawler told us to keep that a secret. We weren't supposed to tell anyone."

"Yeah," Rage says. "Well, that didn't last long."

InvisiBill. You can't tell that big mouth anything.

"Just say he's lying," I say. "Tell them it's not true."

"It's too late," Rage says. "The Howlers already don't believe him."

"Great," I say. "Problem solved. See you in the morning."

"Well," Rage says, "it's not that simple. You see, they dared us to prove it."

"So?" I say. "Ignore them."

"Well, it doesn't quite work like that," Rage says. "You haven't been here for long so you probably haven't learned this yet, but there's an unwritten code of honor here at Monster House. If one team claims something and another team dares them to prove it, you have to prove it. Otherwise, the honor of your entire section is at stake."

"So?" I say. "Who cares?"

"You still don't get it," Rage says. "We have to answer the challenge, otherwise we'll be forced to serve the Howlers for the rest of the term. I don't know about you, but I really don't want to be bringing Blobby breakfast in bed every morning."

Well, I didn't know anything about that.

"And I'm not going to be the one to tell Aura we're not defending our honor," he adds. "The Monstrosities will be laughingstocks all over campus."

"Okay, okay," I say, getting out of bed. Honestly, the last thing I want to do is disappoint Aura again. Defending our honor sounds much easier. "So, what exactly do we have to do?"

"Well," Rage says. "That's the problem. We have to prove what InvisiBill said is true. We have to go into the forbidden basement and prove the Artifacts of Virtue are real."

VAN HELSING ACADEMY

STUDENT ASSESSMENT

VITALS:
NAME: Harper Gale
EYES: Yellow
HAIR: Black
HEIGHT: 4' 11"
WEIGHT: 88 lbs

NOTES: Half-human, half-bird with the wings of a vulture but the body of a girl. Bones are hollow and nails end in razor-sharp talons that can cut through metal.

CODENAME: Harpoon

CLASSIFICATION TYPE:
Abnormal — Harpy

SUPERNATURAL ASSESSMENT:

STRENGTH   ●●○○○
AGILITY   ●●●●○
FIGHTING   ●●●○○
INTELLECT ●●●●●
CONTROL   ●●●●○

TEACHABLE?	Yes	No
VAN HELSING	●	○
CRAWLER	●	○
HOLMWOOD	●	○
SEWARD	●	○
MORRIS	●	○
HEXUM	●	○
~~FAUSTIUS~~	○	○

RISK LEVEL: MEDIUM

CHAPTER SEVEN

THE FORBIDDEN BASEMENT

As Rage and I enter the common room, you could cut the tension with a knife.

The Monstrosities are standing on one side and the Howlers on the other. And smack dab in the middle are Aura and Harpoon, looking like they want to strangle one another.

I'd say this doesn't look good.

"Well, well," Harpoon says, glaring at me with her shifty, yellow eyes. "If it isn't old bat-brain himself. This is great news because if you put him in charge you'll definitely be doing my homework until the end of the term."

The Howlers cackle at my expense. Shocker.

"Where's InvisiBill?" I ask, ignoring them. "Because I'm going to throttle him."

"Take a number," Aura says, not taking her eyes off of Harpoon.

"InvisiBill isn't here anymore," InvisiBill says, his voice coming from somewhere behind us.

"Shut it," Aura and I say at the same time.

"What's going on here?" I ask.

"The Howlers don't believe what InvisiBill—now known as 'the Squealer'—said about the Artifacts of Virtue," Aura says. "And now they've dared us to prove it to them. So, per the Monster House code of honor, we need to cough up the evidence, otherwise, we'll essentially become their servants for life."

"Don't look so pale," Harpoon says with a smile. "Based on the company you're keeping; I'd consider it a major step up the social chain."

Aura crosses her arms and rolls her eyes.

"If they want us to prove it," I say to Aura. "Then let's just prove it."

"Bram," Aura says, shooting me daggers, "don't you remember? The Artifacts of Virtue are hidden in the basement. You know, the basement all students are forbidden to enter."

Oh, yeah.

When I first enrolled in the Van Helsing Academy, Vi Clops warned me never to go into the basement. She said it was 'off limits.' I think her exact words were something like, 'I'd hate for yer to become the second kid in Van Helsing Academy history that gets lost forever on some stupid dare.'

Maybe this is what she was talking about?

But according to Crawler, the Artifacts of Virtue are in the basement. So, if we're going to defend our honor, one or more of us are going to have to go down there.

"I don't care if we lose the dare," Hairball says. "I'm not stepping foot in that basement. I heard there's a monster down there. Like, a really big one."

"Same," Stanphibian says.

"I'm not going either," InvisiBill says.

"What?" Rage says. "But this was all your fault!"

"InvisiBill still isn't here," InvisiBill says.

Surprise, surprise. The three amigos have chickened out. Predictable.

"Fine," Rage says, standing up a bit taller. "I'll do it."

"No, Rage," Aura says firmly. "You're still recovering. I'll go."

"No," I say suddenly, surprising even myself. "I'll do it. I'll go into the basement."

"Whoohoo!" Harpoon yells, pumping her fist. "This is in the bag! Blobby, how do you like your bacon?"

Honestly, I don't want to go, but after everything I've screwed up, I need to prove myself all over again to my team.

"Bram," Aura says, staring at me with her bright, blue eyes. "You don't have to do this. Why don't you stay here and keep an eye on Rage? I've got this."

"No," I say. "I'm going to do it. It's my fault we're out of the Monster Cup in the first place, so I should be the one to go. Besides, it's right up my alley. I can see in the dark, remember? And believe me, you're the only person I trust to keep an eye on Rage tonight. Those were Van Helsing's orders."

"Hey!" Rage says. "I'm not a baby, you know?"

Aura stares at me, waiting for me to fold, but I don't.

"Okay," she finally relents. "It's settled. Bram will go. But only if he really wants to."

"So," I say, turning to Harpoon. "When I find one of these artifacts, how exactly am I supposed to prove to you that it exists? Based on their power, I'm certainly not bringing one back up with me."

"With this camera," Harpoon says, handing me a small, rectangular object. "After all, they say a picture is worth a thousand words."

"Great," I say, taking it from her. It's a small digital camera, about the size of my palm. I open the back cover just to make sure there are batteries inside and then tuck it into one of my hoodie pockets.

"You need to stay alert at all times," Aura says. "It's going to be dangerous."

"That's alright," I say with a wink. "Danger is my middle name."

"Really?" InvisiBill says. "That's funny, for some reason I always thought it was 'Carl.'"

***

Now that it's settled, my first task is to get into the basement. Since I don't know where it is, I'll need Hairball to take me there. And to do that, we'll have to get past Vi Clops—our super-scary cyclops in charge of Monster House. Since Aura has to keep an eye on Rage, I enlist the help of Hairball, Stanphibian, and InvisiBill.

I guess I'll never learn.

The plan is simple. While Stanphibian preoccupies Vi Clops by telling her that he feels sick, InvisiBill will cause a distraction on the other side of the foyer. Then, when Vi Clops goes to investigate, Stanphibian will give a thumbs up when it's all clear, and I'll follow Hairball down the stairs, past Vi Clops' office, and straight to the forbidden basement.

It was foolproof.

Unless, of course, you're working with fools.

"Is InvisiBill in place?" I whisper to Hairball, tapping the staircase banister. I survey the foyer but don't see signs of him anywhere. "He was going to give us a signal when he was in place."

"No clue," Hairball whispers back.

Stanphibian is standing outside Vi Clops' office. He smiles and gives me a thumbs up.

Wait, why is he giving me a thumbs up? I look to the other side for InvisiBill. Did he give a signal?

"Uh-oh," Hairball says.

Uh-oh? Uh-oh, what?

But when I look back down at Stanphibian, I see him entering Vi Clops' office!

"Stan, wait!" Hairball whispers firmly, but Stanphibian has already gone inside.

"What are yer doin' here?" comes Vi Clops' deep, rumbling voice.

Stay calm, Bram. Stanphibian is just going to have to talk for a while until InvisiBill shows up.

Then, I smack my hand into my forehead.

Stanphibian barely ever talks! We're doomed!

Suddenly, someone pushes past me from behind, nearly knocking me down the stairs.

"Sorry," InvisiBill whispers. "Had to make a potty."

"Seriously?" Hairball says.

"Sorry, young one," I hear Vi Clops say. "But I ain't understandin' yer. I'm takin' yer back upstairs to bed."

Oh no! She's coming this way! I try to find

somewhere to hide but my only option is to duck behind Hairball—which isn't an option at all!

Suddenly, I see Vi Clops' large foot in the doorway.

"Follow me," Vi Clops says.

The next thing I know she's standing in the foyer! All twenty feet of her!

CRASH!

The sound of glass shattering echoes through the foyer, and when I look over I see one of the hanging pictures smashed on the floor. The frame is busted and glass is everywhere.

Holy cow! InvisiBill destroyed school property to make a distraction. That's not good.

"What's goin' on?" Vi Clops says, her giant eye darting to the other side of the room. Then, she STOMPS past the stairwell.

Thank goodness! She didn't see us!

I glance back down to find Stanphibian waving at us with his webbed hand. I nod, and Hairball and I race down the stairs and dash under the stairwell through a maze of corridors.

The last time I came this way was when we snuck out of Monster House to stop that grave robbery. I sure hope things work out better this time. I stick close to Hairball as he navigates his way through the seemingly endless twists and turns. Fortunately, he knows this place like the back of his furry hand.

After what feels like hours, we make a final turn, and Hairball stops short in front of a door that would look pretty ordinary if it weren't for the yellow caution tape, multiple locks, and 'DANGER! DO NOT OPEN

UNDER ANY CIRCUMSTANCES!' sign.

"We're here," Hairball says. "You know, in case you didn't notice."

"Oh, I noticed," I say, counting all of the locks. There are five in total.

"Let me break those for you," he says.

But as soon as he reaches for one, I stop him.

"Hold on," I say. "You remember Faustius' door, don't you? I bet these locks are cursed."

"Right," he says. pulling his hand back. "Good call. So, how are you going to get down there then?"

"The vampire way," I say. "Wish me luck."

"You'll need more than luck," Hairball says. "Look, I don't want to freak you out, but I've heard a three-headed monster lives down there. And there is that story about a kid who went down there and was never seen again."

"You know," I say. "I'd appreciate it if you stopped talking now."

"Sorry," he says. "Just want you to be prepared."

"I'm sure it's just an urban legend," I say. But in the pit of my stomach, I'm not so sure. I mean, I've encountered some crazy stuff over the last few months.

"I hope so," Hairball says. "For your sake."

"Gee, thanks," I say. "See you soon."

Then, I focus on becoming a mist. I envision myself as a vapor cloud, flowing seamlessly through the cracks of the door. I hold that vision in my mind, focusing only on that goal, and suddenly, I feel tingly all over.

The next thing I know, my body feels light, like it's pulling itself apart. And then I flow through the cracks of the basement door and collect myself on the other side.

Once I'm pulled together, I focus again on becoming a kid, and when I transform, I'm standing on the top step of an old stone staircase. Well, that was easy. Now I just need to take care of business. But when I look down the staircase, I realize I can't see a thing. It's pitch dark and my eyes don't seem to be adjusting.

Hmmm. That's weird. I blink my eyes a few times and then open them wide, but my vision doesn't change.

What's going on here?

Then, a lightbulb goes off.

If I thought the door was cursed, then I bet the darkness may be a curse too. I bet Van Helsing did that to deter visitors who managed to get past the door. Well, if that's the case, then this is going to be way creepier than I imagined. I sure hope the camera has a powerful flash setting.

Suddenly, my heart drops to my toes.

The camera!

I feel inside my pocket to make sure it's still there and it is. Whew! I didn't realize I could transport objects with me when I went into mist-form, but I guess that's why my clothes stay on my body when I go back to kid-form. I don't understand how that works, but it sure beats standing here naked.

Then, my head bumps into something high against the wall. I lean over and feel it with my hand. It's a lantern. Perfect! I grab it off the hook and turn the dial, and it lights up the space around me. Well, that's helpful. Now I can see a few feet in every direction.

Okay, here goes nothing. I take a deep breath and make my way down the twisting staircase. Judging by the stone walls and dusty floor, this place is really, really old. And about halfway down I notice a hanging wooden sign that reads:

DANGER!
TURN BACK NOW!

Well, that's comforting.

Believe me, I'd love nothing more than to heed that warning, but I know I can't. After all, I don't want to let my team down again. All I need to do is find one of the Artifacts of Virtue hidden somewhere down here and snap a photo. How hard could that be?

It's not until I hit the bottom of the staircase that I have my answer, because I'm standing in the center of a large chamber surrounded by a dozen corridors.

Are you kidding me? Which way am I supposed to go? I turn aimlessly in a circle as a million thoughts fly through my brain at once. Which corridor should I pick first? What if I pick the wrong one? What if I get lost down here forever? What if I die of starvation?

Speaking of starvation, I haven't eaten anything since dinner. Normally, I'd be fine until breakfast, but what if I'm stuck here past breakfast? And if I use my super-speed, I may get through some of these corridors quicker, but I'll just end up making myself weaker.

And that wouldn't be good if there really is a three-headed monster down here.

Okay, get it together. There's no science to this. I'm just going to have to pick a corridor and go for it. I raise my lantern, searching for any clues as to which way to go, but the corridors all look the same.

So, I pick the one straight ahead.

As I move forward, I realize I'm walking through a cold and musty tunnel that looks strangely familiar. Unlit torches hang from the rock walls every ten feet or so and I hear the sound of running water overhead.

That's when it hits me.

This was the tunnel I saw in my dream!

I stoop beneath the low ceiling when my lantern reveals something that makes my heart stop.

Footprints.

Heading in the same direction I'm going.

Someone is down here.

"H-Hello?" I call out, my voice echoing through the tunnel.

Then, I wonder why I did that. I might as well have doused myself in ketchup and told the three-headed monster it was snack time! At this point I could turn back—I probably should turn back—but then I would have failed Aura and the others. So, I take another breath and follow the footprints.

My pace quickens as I weave my way through the tunnel. But it's not until I step directly on one of the footprints that I notice something else.

The footprints match my shoe size.

I shake my head in disbelief. Something is not right, but I can't stop. I need to see where this goes, so I follow the tunnel to the end.

And that's when I see the iron vault door.

And it's wide open.

CLASSIFIED

Person(s) of Interest

CODE NAME: NONE

REAL NAME: VIOLET CLOPS

BASE OF OPERATIONS: VAN HELSING ACADEMY

FACTS: Violet Clops (a.k.a. 'Vi Clops') is the Residence Hall Manager of Monster House — the living quarters for students of the Van Helsing Academy. She is responsible for ensuring the safety of students on campus. Her origin and relationship with Van Helsing is unknown.

FIELD OBSERVATIONS:

- Angers easily
- Incredibly strong
- Requires an extreme number of daily calories
- Falls asleep after consuming large meals

Category: Supernatural

Sub-Type: Cyclops

Height: 20'4"

Weight: 535 lbs

STATUS: ACTIVE TARGET

DEPARTMENT OF SUPERNATURAL INVESTIGATIONS

CHAPTER EIGHT

RATS AGAIN!

I'm in total shock.

The vault door is… open?

And the footprints that led me here match my shoe size exactly! My mind is working on overdrive. I mean, I can't help but put two and two together.

I thought it was all just a bad dream. Yet, the evidence in front of me is telling me something else. I clearly remember walking down this very same tunnel and grabbing the wheel that opens the vault door. I couldn't stop myself. And now that I'm standing here in person, there's no denying it.

It wasn't a dream at all.

Somehow, I must have come down here after helping Rage go to bed. And when he woke me up, I had no clue where I was, yet I was lying in my bed with my shoes on. But how did I even get here? I had no idea where the basement door was even located. I needed Hairball to take me there.

Then, something else makes me shudder.

The voice.

That cold, raspy voice who was trying to convince me to open the door.

The hairs on the back of my neck stand on end.

I-I know that voice.

It-It couldn't be him. But then I remember that flapping sound. And the fact that he called me by my first name. But that's impossible, right?

I mean, if it was him, he was… in my head?

Count Dracula was in my head!

No, it couldn't be. The last time I saw him, he was a shell of himself. His spirit had just been revived inside a mish-mashed skeleton of dead people. He was skin and bones and whiter than a ghost. But it's been months since then. He could be stronger by now. Much stronger.

But why would he come here?

Van Helsing is his greatest enemy. He'd be risking his own life coming to the Van Helsing Academy. But then I remember looking into his red, evil eyes, and watching his mouth curl into a sinister smile as he told me: 'Until next time.'

Does that mean he's coming for me?

I try wiping the thought from my mind, but it won't go away. Suddenly, a burst of cold air blows through the tunnel and I shiver. That's when I notice the vault door swaying on its hinges. Maybe I'm just being paranoid. I mean, I never actually saw Dracula in my dream. Maybe it wasn't him? Maybe my mind is playing tricks on me?

But as I stare into the darkness beyond the open doorframe I get a curious thought.

What's on the other side?

I step towards the dark opening but stop myself. This is all strange enough, do I really need to see what's through the door too? Probably not, but as soon as I take a step backward, my curiosity gets the best of me and I lunge forward, extending the lantern through the doorframe.

SCREEEEECCCHHHH!

Suddenly, a million tiny creatures scatter up and away before my eyes!

I jump back, my heart pumping like crazy, and I barely manage to hang on to the lantern. Those were bugs. Like, lots of bugs. But what were they doing there?

And that's when I notice the door opens into a hollow tree trunk. And in the middle of the tree trunk is an iron ladder, climbing straight up the inside of the twisted, hollowed-out tree!

At first, I'm confused. Then, it clicks.

This hollow tree must be a secret entrance from the outside—right into the basement of the Van Helsing Academy!

I'm shocked. I mean, I didn't know this entrance existed. But someone did. And whoever knew, must have passed that information to Count Dracula!

Okay, I think I've seen enough. So, I step back inside, slam the door closed, and lock the vault door.

Well, I know one thing, no one else is getting in.

But the question is, will I ever get out?

SSSNNAAARRRLLL!

The growl echoes through the tunnel and I spin around, but there's nothing there.

Two thoughts flash through my mind. One, there really is a three-headed monster. And two, the last kid who came down here never made it back.

I feel like I'm gonna puke.

Okay, I didn't want to use my super-speed, but given present circumstances, I may need to rethink my plan. I'm just here to snap a picture of one of the Artifacts of Virtue. I don't care if it's the bell, book, or candle.

But then again, maybe I should just abandon this little dare and get the heck out of here? After all, I'm not interested in becoming someone's lunch. I think the team would forgive me. They wouldn't respect me, but they'd probably forgive me.

Of course, if I did use my super-speed, I could jet through these corridors until I found one of the artifacts and take the stupid picture. But if I run into whatever made that noise, I might not have the strength to fight back. I don't know what to do, but I do know one thing, I can't just stand here.

Just then, I hear pitter-patter noises behind me, like clawed feet walking across a hard surface, followed by—

"…dangerous me said."

"Hear you me do but see if it made it, we must. Then

reward we collect."

I lift my lantern high, and my jaw hits the floor. To my astonishment, I see a tall, thin rat squeezing through a crack in the stone wall. And then I see a second one who is smaller and fatter than the first.

Now, I'm no expert in rat identification, but these two look very, very familiar. And if they are who I think they are, then they owe me big time.

"Done is job," the thin one says. "Me food reward now me want, not danger."

"Well, too bad, that is," I say, speaking in my best Rat. "Because danger you found."

The fat one turns around and his eyes bulge out. "The pink one!" he yells. "Run!"

The fat one takes off, but I'm too fast for the thin one, grabbing him before he knows what hit him.

"Let go!" he yells, trying to sink his claws in my hand.

"Knock it off," I say, tightening my grip. "Or squeeze I will and gone you be."

"Help!" the thin rat yells.

But the fat one just stands there.

"Help me you will," I say. "Or friend goes bye-bye."

"So?" the fat rat says, shrugging his shoulders.

"So!" the thin one says outraged, pointing down at his friend. "Save me you must!"

"Must me?" the fat rat says. "Care me don't. Food more for me."

"What?" the thin rat yells.

But I'm not fooled. These two are partners in crime. According to Van Helsing, they were the ones who sold me out to the Dark Ones after I was dumped into that kid dungeon at the New England School for Troubled Boys. It's funny how long ago that seems now.

Then, I realize something.

If these two are walking around here so casually, they must know about the secret entrance. In fact, I bet they're the ones who sold that information to Count Dracula! And come to think of it, I bet they've also been down here a million times, which means they probably know where other things are located.

Like the Artifacts of Virtue!

But I know they won't just tell me. These guys are mercenaries. If I'm going to get them to take me there, I'm going to have to negotiate a deal—even if I don't intend to hold up my end of the bargain.

"Okay," I say. "No care for life of friend me see. But me have other things you may be interested in, like secrets."

"Secrets?" the fat one repeats, his little ears perking up. "Of secrets what kind?"

"Important secrets," I say. "Secrets worth much food. Much, much, much food. But me no tell. Secrets too important."

"Much, much, much food?" the fat rat says, his voice rising with excitement. "Me your secrets tell?"

Eight

"Play you not," the thin one says. "Pink one me bite now."

But as he opens his mouth, the fat rat and I both yell "No!"

"Fool!" the fat one yells. "No bite Pink One! Pink One has secrets worth much, much, much food. Secrets me want to hear."

"Fine," the thin one says, crossing his arms. "Me want much, much, much food also."

"Tell you me will," I say. "But first me you help."

The fat rat doesn't respond and instead puts his hands on his hips. He looks like a furry teacup, but I can tell his tiny mind is churning. I need to be careful with this guy.

"Okay," he says finally. "Me help you. But then secrets tell you will."

"And me release!" the thin one says. "Me release!"

"Deal," I say. "And me release only after you help."

"Okay," the fat one says. "What you want?"

"Me want you to lead me to bell, book, or candle," I say. "Me know you know where they are."

The two rats look at one another and break out into squeaky laughter.

"What?" I say.

"Nothing," the fat rat says suspiciously. "Show you we will. Hurry but you must."

I nod, and the fat rat takes off like a mini rocket, heading back towards the tunnel entrance. I try to keep up, but the floor is uneven and I don't want to drop the thin rat or the lantern. Plus, I'm keeping a lookout for whatever made that growling noise.

For some reason, heading back seems to take even longer, but then, we suddenly exit the tunnel and I'm back in the main chamber. I'm more than relieved to see the stairwell leading upstairs again, and nearly talk myself into taking it, but I just can't do it. Like it or not, I'm committed to seeing this through.

"Left we go!" yells the thin rat.

"No!" the fat one yells back. "Right it is."

"Right is taken," the thin rat complains.

"Shut your snout," the fat one yells. "Me lead."

"Ohhh," the thin one finally says.

"Um, what's wrong?" I ask the thin rat.

"Oh, nothing," he says casually. "All good."

The fat rat enters the corridor diagonally to the right and I follow, but I can't help but think that something is not 'all good.' The thin one made it sound like we're going the wrong way. And what did he mean by 'it is taken?'

I know I can't trust these rats, but it's not like I've got a choice. Right now, I just have to go with the flow and hope my fake secrets pay off.

As we run through the tunnel, I realize how eerily similar it is to the one we just came out of. I mean, if you weren't keeping track of where you've been, it would be impossible to tell one tunnel from the next. Nevertheless, we travel for what seems like an eternity until we hit a feature that stops us cold—a rock wall blocking our path.

"We here," the fat one says, pointing to the wall. "What seek you be through there."

"But that wall be rock?" I say confused.

"No, Pink One," he says. "Touch."

Since my hands are full, I lift my right leg, but when I try making contact with the rock, my leg passes right through. There's nothing there. It's an illusion!

Of course it is.

This basement has more tricks than a magic shop.

"Now, tell secret," the fat one says.

"And me release," the thin one says.

"Um, no," I say. "Me know not what is back there. You come me with, then me tell secret."

The rats shoot each other another look.

Something is up.

"Very well," the fat one says. "Follow." Then, he darts straight through the imaginary rock wall.

I'm about to grill the thin one but he turns the other way. Okay, he's not giving up any info. Well, here goes nothing. I take a deep breath and then step through the rock wall.

When we come out the other side I do a double take, because we're no longer standing in a narrow tunnel, but rather in a large, stone chamber. And in the center of the chamber is a white pedestal, which is holding a green, glowing object.

"The Bell of Virtue!" I exclaim.

I-I can't believe it. It's real!

It's shaped like an upside-down cup, with an ornate handle that looks like a serpent wrapped around a pole. And the whole thing is surrounded by a translucent green glow. I can't take my eyes off of it.

"Now secret!" the fat rat demands.

"Right," I say, snapping back to reality.

Well, to my surprise, the rats delivered on their promise. Unfortunately, I've got nothing for them. I guess they can consider it payback for what they did to me. All I need to do now is get a picture.

I bend over and put down the thin rat and the lantern. He immediately runs over to the fat one and bops him on the head.

"Hate you me do!" he says.

"Ow!" the fat one says, rubbing his noggin. "Now secret!" he demands.

"Sorry," I say, fishing in my pocket for my camera, "but there is no secret. Thanks for bringing me here. Now run along while you still have the chance."

"No secret!" they yell.

"Surprising not." the thin one says with a chuckle. "Pink One think he fool us. But me fool him." And then he pulls out a camera from behind his back.

Huh? Wait a second.

I reach into my pockets again, but my camera is gone! That rat stole my camera!

The rats start cackling again.

"You fool," the thin one says. "Now you fight for life."

Fight for my life? What's he talking about?

GRRRRRRRRR!

Then, something leaps over my head and lands in a crouched position in front of the pedestal!

"Luck good!" the fat one yells.

"No, luck bad!" the thin one yells. "Luck very bad!"

And as the rats scamper off with my camera, the creature in front of me rises and fixes me with its red, luminous eyes.

I stumble backward in shock.

I-I can't believe it.

It's… Tiger-boy?

CHAPTER NINE

FOR WHOM THE BELL TOLLS

I don't know what's worse, facing an angry tiger-kid or being outwitted by a pair of rats!

Well, I've got to hand it to them, those annoying vermin got me again. They knew Tiger-boy was hanging out in this chamber, and now they've run off with my camera, ending my chance to prove the Artifacts of Virtue are real.

Awesome.

After all of this effort, I'll have absolutely nothing to show for it when I get back. Of course, there's still the open question if I'll even make it back. After all, Tiger-boy is standing between me and the Bell of Virtue, looking none too pleased to see me.

What I can't figure out is what he's doing here in the first place? Did he come through the vault door? And if so, why?

"You know," I say, "we've got to stop meeting like this."

"GRRRRR," he responds.

Nine

"Okay, okay," I say, raising my hands and taking a step back. "No need to get testy."

But then I realize something.

Crawler said the Artifacts of Virtue guard the academy from evil. He said that nothing evil at heart could step inside their protective barrier. So, if the Bell of Virtue hasn't moved from its pedestal, and the Tiger-boy is standing here, then maybe he's not evil at all?

I mean, he's not attacking me now, and he didn't attack me at Moreau Labs either. The only thing he did there was point me to Cat-girl.

So, if he's not evil, then maybe he's good?

I stare into his red-eyes and flash a friendly smile.

"I just want you to know," I say, "that we are taking good care of your friend."

His eyes widen, and that's when I notice he actually looks worse than before. His wheezing seems louder, and he's got more bare patches in his fur.

"We brought her here," I continue. "To the school up above. She's getting cared for by one of the best doctors in the world. She's doing much better."

Tiger-boy opens his mouth to speak, but only a small growl comes out.

"We can help you too," I offer, stepping closer to him. "If you want."

"SNARRRRLLL!" he growls.

I freeze. Well, clearly he doesn't want our help.

"Okay," I say. "No problem. Can you at least tell me

who you are? Or what you're even doing here? If you want to see your friend I can take you to her."

I wait for some kind of response, but he just stares at me. And as I look into his eyes, I feel like he's trying to tell me something. I just don't know what. Maybe I'll try again.

"Are you sure you don't want help?" I ask, slowly stepping towards him. "I have friends that can help you. Like Headmaster Van Helsing. He'll be happy to—"

RRROOOAAARRR!

I cover my ears but his growl is deafening, echoing through the chamber. And then, to my surprise, he snatches the Bell of Virtue from the pedestal!

"Wait!" I yell. "What are you—"

But before I can finish my sentence, he jumps over my head and bounds through the rock wall illusion! For a nano-second I'm stunned, and then realization sets in. He just swiped the Bell of Virtue!

Without the bell, the school will lose its Supernatural protection from evil. I've got to stop him!

I turn on super-speed mode and dash after him, but he's nowhere to be seen. I mean, I'm fast but he seems to be even faster! And as I race through the tunnel, the only thing going through my mind is that I blew it.

I'm the one who left the vault door open. I'm the one who failed to stop Tiger-boy. I'm the one who put the whole school in danger.

Suddenly, I exit the tunnel back into the central

chamber. I see the stairwell leading upstairs and the eleven other corridors. I spin around, searching for some clue as to which way he went. I scan the floor for footprints, pawprints, any prints, but I don't see anything! And I'm so turned around I can't even figure out which tunnel leads back to the vault door. Suddenly, I hear—

SCREECH!

SLAM!

And after the echo subsides, there's nothing.

Tiger-boy went out the vault door!

He escaped.

And now there's nothing left to do but go upstairs and face the music.

***

Van Helsing's face hasn't moved a muscle.

I mean, I just spent the last thirty minutes telling him all about the Howlers' dare, my venture into the forbidden basement, and how Tiger-boy ran off with the Bell of Virtue—and all he did was stare at me.

Honestly, I don't even know if Van Helsing is still breathing, but now that I've finished my tale, he hasn't said a word. Instead, we're all just sitting in his office in awkward silence. The Monstrosities are here, along with Crawler, and all I want to do is jump into Van Helsing's raging fire.

And while Van Helsing's face is a study in stone,

Crawler's eyes are practically bugging out of his head. I already felt guilty enough, but now I feel even worse since I'll probably get Crawler in trouble for telling us about the Artifacts of Virtue in the first place.

I try reading Van Helsing's steely expression to guess what he's thinking. The last time we got in major trouble he let us set our own punishments. Something tells me he might think differently this time. Especially after listening to what I had to say.

I mean, I pretty much told him everything, including being tricked by those rats, which I admit wasn't one of my finer moments.

But there were a few things I left out.

With everyone standing here, I couldn't find the courage to tell him about my 'dream' that wasn't really a dream at all. And I sort of left out the part about me being the one who opened the vault door. I couldn't even imagine my team's reaction if I dropped that stink bomb.

I mean, what would they think of me then?

Honestly, I'm not even sure what I think of me right now. Between this blunder and nearly drinking Rage's blood, I feel like I'm totally losing control of myself.

And I'm scared.

I rub my eyes with my palms.

I don't know what to do next.

"We are all in grave danger," Van Helsing says suddenly, snapping me back to attention.

"Here we go," InvisiBill says.

"The Artifacts of Virtue only work as a unit," Van Helsing continues. "Removing one negates the power of all. They were passed down to me from my grandfather, Abraham Van Helsing, who stumbled across their legend in ancient texts while researching methods to defeat Count Dracula. My grandfather had to overcome great personal danger to recover each artifact, which had been scattered across the globe."

"I'm so sorry," I say.

"It is not your fault," Van Helsing says. "Clearly, Count Dracula learned the Supernatural objects were here, protecting the academy from his influence, and he executed a plan to remove this barrier."

But Van Helsing doesn't understand. It was my fault. And according to what he just said that voice on the other side of the door must have been Count Dracula after all!

I feel like I'm gonna puke.

"Wait," Rage says. "Are you saying that Count Dracula could now come on campus?"

"Yes," Van Helsing says. "He is free to walk the grounds, but there is one limit to his reach. As long as you remain indoors, you may be safe, for a vampire must be invited inside a building to gain entry. But that rule does not apply to his minions."

Well, there's something else I just learned. I didn't realize a vampire needed an invitation just to enter a building. But I guess that doesn't apply to me because I'm half-human. I have no problem going in and out of places.

"But here's something I don't get," Aura says. "How did that tiger-dude get in the basement anyway? If the Artifacts of Virtue were doing their job, then I thought evil couldn't step foot on school grounds?"

"An excellent question," Van Helsing says. "But I believe there is only one possible explanation. The perpetrator was likely not evil at heart. Only truly dark souls cannot breach the Artifacts' protective barrier. Those who are not evil, but merely misguided, are not impeded."

So, I was right. Tiger-boy isn't evil.

"Wait," Hairball says. "I don't understand. If the tiger-kid isn't a bad guy, then why did he steal the bell?"

"Count Dracula is a master of manipulation," Van Helsing says. "Who knows what he promised the child in exchange for the Bell of Virtue? But whatever it was, clearly it was motivation enough. We may never know the answer."

"Well, I know how to get some answers," Aura says. "Let's go wake up Cat-girl. I bet she knows what's going on. Come to think of it, I bet she's the one who opened the vault door in the first place."

"Yeah!" Stanphibian says unexpectedly.

"No," Van Helsing says. "We will not subject that poor child to additional trauma. She is still recovering from her time in Dr. Moreau's clutches. When she comes to, we will gain more answers if she has them. But until then, we will continue to operate under our mission as a sanctuary for monster children. Is that understood?"

"Yes," Aura mutters, reluctantly.

As Van Helsing looks us in the eyes, I feel relief. I mean, I wouldn't want that girl to be blamed for something I did. And if Van Helsing hadn't stepped in, I'd be forced to tell everyone that I was the one who opened the door. I know I'll tell them eventually, but first I need to figure some things out.

Like, what's wrong with me?

"Monstrosities," Van Helsing says, "I would like to thank you all for bringing this situation to my attention. We will discuss your punishment when I return."

"Punishment?" InvisiBill says. "But we told you everything."

"As I expect you would," Van Helsing says, tightening his scarf. "But we cannot forget your actions violated our rules. Therefore, we will discuss the consequences at another time. At the moment, we have a bell to recover."

"We'll come too," Aura says, clenching her fists.

"No," Van Helsing says. "All of you will be going back to Monster House to await instructions from Professor Hexum. I will be leading a small team in pursuit of the tiger boy. Based on Bram's account of his agility, he is likely far away by now. But we should be able to pick up his trail and track him to his destination."

"Um, didn't you say it's not safe here anymore?" Hairball asks.

"That is true," Van Helsing says. "But it is much safer if you are all together under the watchful eye of our faculty. Crawler, can you please collect Professor Morris and get ready for our journey? And please ask Professor Hexum to wait outside my office."

"Yes, Headmaster," Crawler says, heading out, but not before shooting me a disappointed look.

"As for the rest of you," Van Helsing says. "I will notify Professor Holmwood, Professor Seward, Mrs. Clops, and Dr. Renfield to collect you and your fellow students at Monster House. I expect all of you to follow their instructions without exception. You are all dismissed. Except for Bram."

As I watch the others file out with their heads hanging low, I shift nervously in my chair. This is not going to be good. I mean, I crossed the line the most by actually going into the forbidden basement. Van Helsing has to be royally upset with me.

It's only after the door to his office finally shuts that he looks at me and says—

"Your life is at risk."

"W-What?" I say, swallowing hard. Of all the things I thought he'd say, I certainly wasn't expecting that.

"Your life is at risk," he repeats. "With the removal of the Bell of Virtue, the academy is no longer a safe haven for you. Now, nothing is stopping Count Dracula and his minions from coming onto campus and attacking you."

My stomach drops.

"So," I say, "are you telling me Count Dracula had the bell stolen just to… kill me?"

"Possibly," Van Helsing says. "After all, you are the only thing standing between him and immortality. Remember, only a vampire can truly kill another vampire. A fatal blow from one vampire to another will not only destroy his mortal body, but his spirit as well, and that is the only way he will forever cease to exist. And as far as I am aware, you are the only two vampires left in existence."

"B-But," I stammer, "won't he make more vampires? Isn't that what vampires do?"

"Dracula is many things," Van Helsing says, "but he is no fool. Since his reemergence, I have monitored the globe for reports of new vampires. But to my surprise, there has been nothing. That tells me he has finally learned his lesson."

"Lesson?" I say. "What lesson?"

"That creating more vampires merely creates more enemies who could destroy him," Van Helsing says. "Dracula is still weak, and he will not compromise his existence. I believe he is living off of animal blood for the time being, but that does not make you any safer."

"Well," I say, feeling more panicked by the second, "if I'm not safe here, where should I go?"

"Nowhere," Van Helsing says, rising from his chair and picking up his Crossbow of Purity.

"Um, really?" I say. "But you just said I'm not safe here?"

"You are not safe anywhere," he says. "But you also cannot afford to waste time traveling from town to town like a nomad. Here you can continue your training immediately under the supervision of Professor Hexum and Dr. Renfield. They will be by your side at all times, helping you to become both physically and mentally stronger for a possible encounter with Count Dracula."

"O-Okay," I mutter.

I can't believe this.

"Now I must go," Van Helsing says, putting his hand on my shoulder. "To protect us all, we must find the Bell of Virtue as quickly as possible. Do you understand everything I have told you?"

"Y-Yes," I stammer.

"Very well," he says. "Professor Hexum will be waiting outside my door for you. You must focus day and night on becoming the most powerful vampire you can be. Good luck, Bram."

"Y-Yeah," I manage to say. "You too."

But as he exits, my mind is focused on only one terrible image.

Count Dracula.

CHAPTER TEN

THAT'S JUST FANGTASTIC

"He will destroy you!"

I hear Hexum's voice in the distance, but I don't want to listen. I'm in full bat-form, gliding through the air without the greatest of ease. He's been putting me through death-defying drills for hours, and quite frankly I'm exhausted. But he promised me this is the last one, so I'm gonna go with that.

I turn the corner and swoop down over the target, a yellow number 2 pencil. All I have to do is pick it up with my little bat feet and fly back to Hexum before the timer runs out.

It sounds easy.

Unless, of course, someone is firing arrows at you.

THWIP!

I flap hard, lifting myself up just as the arrow zips by, its feathers brushing my derriere. Whew! That was way too close for comfort. I can't believe Van Helsing left me in the care of this psycho.

This time, Hexum is training me to sharpen my

radar—and I can tell you it's working on overdrive! I send my signals out again.

THWIP! THWIP!

Two more arrows! Heading straight for my wings!

I rotate sideways and suck in my gut as the arrows whizz past on each side. Thank goodness I had a light lunch. But this guy is nuts!

His training is going to kill me!

I set myself over the pencil and drop down, wrapping my feet around its hexagonal barrel. Then, I pull up into the air.

Time to end my torture once and for all.

I spot Hexum at the far end of the gymnasium. He's leaning on his walking stick and looking at his watch. I had one minute to get the job done and based on all of the time I used dodging killer arrows, I'm pretty sure I'm right on the bubble. But now I should be in the clear.

I'm going to make it.

I pulse out my radar one last time but nothing pings back, except for a strange reading from the pencil I'm carrying. It seems... bigger? And when I look down, I'm no longer holding a yellow pencil, but a dark green snake with yellow bands running down its body!

It's a King Cobra!

SSSSSSSSSS!

AAAAHHH!

I open my toes and the snake plummets. But right before it hits the floor it turns back into a pencil!

"Time!" Hexum barks, as I fly over his head.

What happened? I land on the ground and focus on becoming a kid again, transforming back to my normal self. Then, I look at Hexum's smug face and I realize he's tricked me again. That pencil was never a snake. And those arrows weren't real either. Hexum put all of those things in my mind.

"You failed, Mr. Murray," Hexum says. "When will you learn that your mind is your weakest instrument. If you are easily tricked, you will be easily defeated."

"What can I say? You got me," I admit.

"I did," Hexum says. "But luckily for you, I am only your teacher. Count Dracula is your enemy. His powers of deception are legendary, and he will show you no mercy. If you are going to defeat him, you will need to harden your mind to see beyond the obvious. Shall we try again?"

"No!" I say, with more passion than I intended. "I mean, sorry, but I'm just... tired. And you promised that was the last one. Can't we take a break? Please?"

Hexum stares at me for a few seconds, drumming his fingers on the silver cap of his walking stick.

"Very well," he says. "It appears to be Dr. Renfield's shift anyway. I guess time does fly when you're having fun. Good evening, Mr. Murray. And good luck."

Good luck? What's that supposed to mean.

But I guess I won't have to wait long to find out, because as soon as Hexum leaves, Dr. Renfield enters the gymnasium. He smiles when he sees me and I instantly get a case of the heebie-jeebies.

I don't know why this guy creeps me out so much. Maybe it's because he put me in a trance and embarrassed me in front of the whole class. Or maybe it's because he seemed so excited to study me like I was some kind of a lab animal. I don't know what it is, but there's something strange about him.

"You must be tired, Mr. Murray," he says, walking towards me. "But don't worry, we won't be doing anything physical this evening. That is Professor Hexum's area of expertise. Headmaster Van Helsing has tasked me with helping you to better understand yourself."

"Can't I just hang out with my friends?" I ask. "I haven't seen them in a while and I just want to relax."

"Unfortunately, no," he says. "It is a dangerous time, Mr. Murray. And right now, relaxation is a luxury you cannot afford."

"So, you think Dracula is coming for me also, don't you?" I ask, my voice rising. "Hexum is convinced he is."

"Shall we sit?" Dr. Renfield suggests.

Why not? I guess I'm gonna be here a while, so I nod and plop myself down on the gym floor. Dr. Renfield follows, positioning himself directly across from me.

"Now, to answer your question," he says. "Yes, I do believe it is likely. But I also know there are other things here at the Van Helsing Academy that are of great interest to him. However, if you are his true target, then you must be prepared to defend yourself. Now, shall we begin?"

"Hang on," I say. "Are you saying I might not be his target? That there are other things here that interest him more? Like, what kinds of things?"

"Oh, I do not think that is very important right now," Dr. Renfield says dismissively. "We should use our time more wisely."

"No," I insist. "I think I have a right to know."

Dr. Renfield looks hesitant to tell me, but right now I'll take any reason for why Dracula wants to invade the school as long as it isn't me.

"Very well," Dr. Renfield says. "But after this, we will have to begin."

"Okay," I say. "Sounds fair."

"How should I start?" he asks. "Well, you are aware that Headmaster Van Helsing is a collector of Supernatural lore. After all, you have seen his Crossbow of Purity and, of course, the Bell of Virtue. But it is rumored that Van Helsing also possesses many other Supernatural artifacts—one of which is of particular interest to Count Dracula."

"Really?" I say, my curiosity peaked. "What is it?"

Dr. Renfield peers over his shoulder to ensure the coast is clear, and then he looks back at me. I lean forward, eager for him to tell me, but I can see he's not quite sure if he should say anything. I need to convince him.

"I swear," I say, putting my hand over my heart. "I

won't tell anybody. I'll keep it to myself."

"Very well," Dr. Renfield says. "It is an object of great power. An object known as the Spear of Darkness."

The Spear of Darkness?

Why does that sound so familiar? Then, it clicks. I vaguely remember Professor Seward talking about it in his Supernatural History class.

"Based on your expression," Dr. Renfield says, "it looks like you have heard of it?"

"Yes," I say. "I mean, I've heard its name mentioned before in class. What does it do?"

"According to ancient scriptures," he says, "the Spear of Darkness gives the one wielding it the power to blanket the sky in a shroud of darkness, blotting out the sun."

"Blotting out the sun?" I say. "You mean, like, getting rid of daylight?"

"That is correct," Dr. Renfield says. "As you know all too well, sunlight is the enemy of the vampire. When vampires are directly exposed to sunlight for an extended period, their mortal bodies will be destroyed by the light. That is why Count Dracula operates only at night. Now, imagine a world without daylight? There will be nothing stopping Count Dracula from terrorizing the innocent at all hours, day and night. He will grow stronger faster, quickly becoming unstoppable."

I swallow hard.

I mean, I know exactly what he's talking about. My

skin burns easily when I'm exposed to sunlight, but I never imagined that anything could blot out the sun. I guess it would solve my sunburn problems, but that's just being selfish. There's no way I'd ever want Count Dracula roaming around uninhibited.

"You can see why obtaining the Spear of Darkness would be so valuable to Count Dracula," Dr. Renfield says. "But unfortunately, I do not know if it is truly here at the Van Helsing Academy or not. I was unable to ask Headmaster Van Helsing about it before he left, but if it is here, it will be up to us to protect it from Count Dracula and his minions, just as we need to protect you."

"Yeah," I say. "I would think so."

"If we only knew where it is hiding…" Dr. Renfield says, his voice trailing off. "Did Van Helsing ever discuss the Spear of Darkness with you—even as just a passing comment?"

"No," I say, wracking my brain, but I don't remember anything. "He's never mentioned it."

"Are you sure?" Dr. Renfield presses. "After all, this is very important. I'm sure he must have mentioned it at least one time. You just have to think harder."

"Um, okay," I say. I mean, I know finding the Spear of Darkness is important and all, but it's not like my answer is going to change.

But as I look into Dr. Renfield's eyes I realize I might have been wrong about him. After all, Van Helsing clearly trusts him, and it seems like he wants to stop

Count Dracula as badly as I do. So, maybe my first impression was wrong? Maybe I can put my trust in him?

"Dr. Renfield," I say. "I know you're an expert in what makes monsters tick, so I was wondering if you could, well, help me out. You see, some strange things have been happening to me lately. But I don't want to do the hypnosis thing, like, ever again."

"Of course, Mr. Murray," Dr. Renfield says, his eyebrows rising. "We don't have to use hypnosis. Why don't we just talk?" Then, he reaches into his shirt pocket and pulls out a tiny pad and a pen. "Please, tell me."

I consider telling him about my weird 'dream' but change my mind. Instead, I decide to tell him about the other thing that's been bothering me.

"Well," I say, "there was a situation where one of my friends was injured, and he was bleeding, and…"

I stop. This is just so embarrassing.

"Yes," Dr. Renfield says, encouraging me. "Please, go on. Do not worry. I have heard it all. I will not judge you."

"Well, okay," I say, feeling a little better about sharing. "I-I had this incredible urge to drink his blood. I-I didn't, but it was kind of hard not to. But it worries me. A lot."

"Worries you in what way?" Dr. Renfield asks, his voice sounding calm and even, like what I'm telling him isn't something to be worried about at all.

"Well," I say, "I-I've never wanted to drink anyone's

blood before. I mean, I only eat red food, but never blood. I-I just hope I'm not turning into a… a…"

"Vampire?" Dr. Renfield says, finishing my sentence for me. "But you are a vampire, Mr. Murray."

"No," I say. "I'm a half-vampire. My father was a vampire but my mother was human."

"Yes, of course," he says. "But as you get older, your father's vampire genes will likely try to dominate over your mother's human genes. This is not unusual when it comes to monster biology. In fact, it has been scientifically proven that Supernatural cells divide far more quickly than Natural cells. And as your Natural cells die through damage or aging, they are replaced by more and more Supernatural cells. Thus, over time, the molecular structure of your body will become less Natural and more Supernatural. And this transition will gradually impact your thoughts and behaviors."

Um, what?

My jaw is hanging open, because based on what he just said, my desire to drink Rage's blood wasn't a fluke at all, but rather a result of me becoming more and more of a vampire every single day!

I'm totally speechless.

"I know this is shocking information to absorb," Dr. Renfield says. "But based on what you have described, it appears to fit your situation. Do not despair. Not all half-breeds end up fully embracing their Supernatural side. A handful that I have studied were able to control their monster instincts and live relatively normal lives."

"That's great for them," I say. "But didn't you tell me you've never studied a vampire before?"

"Well," he says. "That is a fair point."

My mind is totally spinning right now.

Because now I not only have to stop Count Dracula, but I may need to stop myself!

I mean, I can't become a full-fledged vampire!

BOOM!

Suddenly, the gym doors fly open and Rage is standing in the doorway with a bizarre look on his face. It's great to see him, but what's he doing here? I thought he was being watched by the other professors with the rest of the kids in the auditorium.

"Bram! Dr. Renfield!" he yells. "Come quick!"

"Why?" I ask. "What's going on?"

"You've got to hurry!" he yells back. "Cat-girl finally woke up!"

CLASSIFIED

Person(s) of Interest

CODE NAME: None

REAL NAME: ALASTAIR HEXUM

BASE OF OPERATIONS: VAN HELSING ACADEMY

FACTS: Alastair Hexum is the tenured Professor of Survival Skills at the Van Helsing Academy. He is a powerful mentalist with the unique ability to tap into a person's mind and alter their sense of reality. He is considered extremely dangerous and should not be confronted alone.

Category: Unknown

Sub-Type: Unknown

Height: 6'2"

Weight: 213 lbs

FIELD OBSERVATIONS:

- Sustained an unknown leg injury requiring use of a walking stick

- Extremely clever and highly observant

- Unpopular among his colleagues and students due to his abrasive personality

STATUS: ACTIVE TARGET

DEPARTMENT OF SUPERNATURAL INVESTIGATIONS

[108]

CHAPTER ELEVEN

THE TRUTH HURTS

By the time we reach the infirmary, I'm ready to check myself into the psychiatric ward.

I mean, Dr. Renfield basically told me the reason I wanted to suck Rage's blood is because my body is attacking itself! He said the vampire cells inside of me are slowly taking over the human cells inside of me. And if it continues at this pace, it'll only be a matter of time before I'm a full-fledged vampire!

The very thought makes me shudder.

I mean, what if I can't control myself?

"Through here," Rage says, entering the infirmary.

I follow him inside when it hits me. What if I become the vampire version of Rage? I mean, Rage loses all control when he turns into a purple monster. He has absolutely no clue where he's been or what he's done. If I become a full vampire and that happens to me, then no one around me is safe.

And what's even scarier is that I have no clue when this might happen. Who knows? It could take years or it could happen in a few hours. It's not like some alarm clock is going to go off telling me time's up. I could slip at any moment, but I know one thing, I will never put innocent lives in danger. No matter what.

"Over here," Rage says, snapping me back to reality.

As he passes through the reception area into the medical wing, I hold the door open for Dr. Renfield, who arrives huffing and puffing behind us from the long run over. Once he gets to the door, I catch up to Rage.

I've never seen the infirmary this empty before. But other than Rage, I guess all of the other kids are still in the auditorium. Well, all except for one, because floating inside one of the patient rooms is a very angry-looking ghost girl.

"It's about time you got here," Aura says. "Because I was just about to ask her the tough questions."

I look down at the infirmary bed to find the subject of Aura's interrogation staring back at me. It's Cat-girl, and she's awake! For the first time, I see her green, cat-like eyes, and it's clear she'd rather be anywhere else than here.

"Not so fast," Dr. Hagella says, entering the room with Dr. Renfield. "No one gave you permission to be in here. And now that our new friend has just woken up, she'll need some space to recover."

"Recover?" Aura says. "The only thing we should be trying to 'recover' right now is the Bell of Virtue her tiger-buddy stole."

"Tiger-buddy?" Cat-girl says, sitting up. "Peter? Is he here? Where is he?"

"Peter?" Aura says. "Who's Peter?"

"Then, he's not here," Cat-girl says, slumping back down into the bed.

"Um, sorry," Aura says. "But what are you even talking about?"

"Aura, please," Dr. Renfield says, holding up his right hand. "Give her a moment. I know we all would like answers, but she has been through quite a difficult experience." Then, he looks at Cat-girl and says, "Why don't we start with something simple? Can you tell us your name?"

"My... name?" she says. "Yes, I-I'm Katherine, but you can call me Kat. Or at least I was before all of this happened." Then, she runs her hand through her whiskers.

"Do you remember what happened?" I ask. "I mean if it isn't too hard to talk about."

"I... I remember some of it," Kat says, her brow furrowed. "But there are... gaps."

"That is quite alright," Dr. Renfield says, soothingly. "Just tell us what you can remember. Take as much time as you need."

Take as much time as you need? At first, I want to argue that we're running out of time. But then I remember Dr. Renfield is an expert in this area. If this is the pace he wants her to go at, it's probably for a good reason. But when I look over at Aura, she's tapping her foot impatiently.

"Okay," Kat says. "I'll… tell you what I remember. You see, we've always struggled. The 'we' being my twin brother and me. His name is Peter. Well, our dad died when we were young, and our mom held down three jobs just to make ends meet. Peter and I tried to help out where we could, but it was never enough. And then our mom met a new man. He wasn't a nice guy and treated us badly. Peter tried to stand up to him, but they had a big fight. And then…"

As her voice falls off, tears well up in her eyes.

"Do not worry," Dr. Renfield says, putting his hand on her arm. "You are doing just fine. Please continue."

"Well, after that, Peter said he was going to run away. He said he'd rather live on the streets than live in our house. I tried changing his mind, but I couldn't. He was set on leaving, but I couldn't let him go alone. I mean, he's like my other half. We've done everything together our whole lives. So, I knew I had to go with him, and later that night we left."

I swallow hard. Hearing her story reminds me so much of my own. There were so many foster homes I left in the middle of the night because I wasn't being treated right. Except, I was alone. At least they had each other.

"We went as far away as we could go," she says. "But we're just kids. We didn't have any money. We spent all of our time looking for food and finding safe places to sleep. I remember one time we even saw our faces on a 'Missing Persons' flier. I told him that maybe we should go back, but Peter just laughed and said, 'Are you kidding? Look, we're famous!'"

"Maybe we were, but we were also scared. But I couldn't just leave him out there. He's my brother, and I was going to protect him no matter what. And then, one night when we were in some back-alley looking for loose change, he… found us."

"Who?" Rage blurts out, totally enraptured by her story. "Who found you?"

"A man," she says. "He was dressed in all white, from his hat to his suit to his shoes. And parked behind him was an expensive-looking car with its own driver. Clearly, the man was rich, and at first, I wasn't sure he was even talking to us, but we were the only ones in the alley. He had gray eyes and a kind smile. He said we needed help, and he would be willing to help us if we would help him with a special project he was working on. He offered to feed us and let us stay in his home for as long as we wanted. It sounded great, but there was something about him I didn't trust. But Peter was so hungry he accepted the man's offer on the spot."

"You mean, you went with him?" Aura asks.

"Yeah," Kat says, lowering her head, "and it was the worst mistake of our lives. The man took us to his home way up at the top of a mountain. At first, he was very kind. He said we should call him 'Doctor,' and his staff served us a feast. I thought it was strange that their faces were covered except for their eyes, but I didn't dwell on it. Peter ate until he felt like his stomach would burst, but I only ate a little. And then the Doctor showed us to our room and we slept for what seemed like days. But when we woke up everything… changed."

"Please continue," Dr. Renfield says. "I know this is difficult for you, but you are doing great."

"O-Okay," she says. "Well, when I woke up, I was in a cage. Of course, I thought I was dreaming. I mean, what would I be doing inside a cage? But then I noticed another cage across the way, and inside was a large cat. At first, I could only see its head and I thought it was a tiger. That is, until the animal moved and I realized it wasn't a tiger at all because it had the body of a boy. I was horrified and convinced myself I was having a nightmare. But when the boy rolled over and I saw what he was wearing, I knew instantly it wasn't a nightmare at all. It was Peter."

As I listen to the emotion in her voice, the hairs on the back of my neck stand on end.

"Suddenly, I felt sick," she says. "And when I looked down at my own body, my arms and legs were covered in white fur, and I had a tail. Then, I caught my reflection and saw my whiskers. Somehow, I was also part-cat, but not as extreme as Peter. I called out to him, and he heard me, gripping the bars of his cage with his paws. But when he called back, his voice was nothing but a howl. And that's when I knew what had happened."

By now, tears are running down her cheeks so I grab a tissue and hand it to her.

"Thanks," she says, wiping her eyes. "The 'Doctor' had used us for his 'special project.' He tainted the food he fed us with something that transformed us into... this. Because Peter ate more than me, his transformation was more complete. I still looked partly human. I could still speak with words. But Peter was gone—except for his heart. I could tell he was still in there somewhere, fighting to get out."

"I'm so sorry," I say. "But this 'Doctor,' did you ever find out his real name?"

"Yes," she says. "His name was Moreau."

My heart skips a beat.

"Moreau?" Rage says. "That animal!"

"Everyone stay calm," Dr. Renfield says. "Let her tell the rest of her story."

"I-I don't remember it all," she says. "But I do remember Dr. Moreau telling us that he was proud of us. He said we had been the only ones who had gone through this type of transformation and had survived, but it was unlikely we would live for long. He said our bodies would give out under the stress of our new forms. But he could help us. He said he had an antidote."

"An antidote?" Rage says. "What's that?"

"It is a way to reverse a process," Dr. Renfield says. "A way to change them back to their human forms. Did

Dr. Moreau show you this antidote?"

"Yes," she says. "He held it up. It was a red liquid in some kind of vial. There wasn't much of it, and I begged him to give it to Peter, but he just laughed at me. He said he couldn't just give it to us, he said we had to earn it."

"What?" I say. "Earn it, how?"

"By retrieving one of three objects," she says. "hidden in the basement of a school."

"The Artifacts of Virtue!" I blurt out.

"Yes," she says. "That's what he called them. He said if we brought one of them back, he would give us the antidote. Then, he showed us a map. He circled the location of the school as well as an abandoned building where he said we could sleep for the night. After that, he released us into the wild. Things started fine. But after a while, I was having difficulty keeping up. I felt so tired I just needed to sleep. And then I remember feeling dizzy, and that's all I remember up until right now."

"Well, that explains a lot," Aura says.

I nod in agreement, but deep inside I know it doesn't explain everything. Like, what happened in my dream for instance.

"Where am I?" Kat asks, looking around.

"You are at the Van Helsing Academy," Dr. Renfield says. "The same school that Dr. Moreau identified on his map."

"Yeah," Aura says suspiciously. "And your brother stole the Bell of Virtue."

"He did?" Kat says, her eyes lighting up. "That means he'll get the antidote!"

"That's great for him," Aura says. "But he's also put everyone on campus in danger."

"What?" Kat says. "What are you talking about? Peter would never put anyone in danger. He's not like that."

"I hear what you're saying," Aura says. "But we don't know your brother. Or you for that matter."

"Aura, chill," I interject. "I believe what she's saying. If her brother had bad intentions, he would have attacked me down in the basement. But he didn't."

"Wait," Kat says, looking at me. "You saw him? You saw Peter?"

"Yes," I say. "Twice actually. In the basement, and before that at Moreau Labs where we found you. Actually, your brother wanted us to find you. That's when you blacked out. I guess Peter knew we could help you."

"Or," Aura says, her eyes narrowing, "her brother knew we went to the Van Helsing Academy. And this was one big set-up to get little Miss Cat-girl here inside the gates so she could open the vault door for him."

"I didn't think of that!" Rage says.

"What vault door?" Kat asks.

"Don't play dumb," Aura says, pressing harder. "Come on! Admit it! You set us up!"

"No!" I say, surprising even myself. I mean, I didn't want to tell them about the vault door yet, but I can't just stand here and let Kat take the blame for something I did. "She didn't do it. I was the one who opened the vault door."

"What?" Aura and Rage say in unison.

"I did it," I say. "It was me. At first, I thought it was just a strange dream. But as I was walking through that tunnel I realized it wasn't a dream at all. Somehow, I had come down that tunnel before and opened the vault door."

"Mr. Murray?" Dr. Renfield says, his eyebrows raised in surprise. "Are you certain?"

"Yes," I say. "Very certain."

I look up ashamed. Everyone is staring at me and the room is so quiet you could hear a pin drop. I blink and my eyelashes feel damp. Great, now I'm gonna cry.

"Bram," Dr. Hagella says, reaching for my arm, but I pull away. I just want to get out of here.

"AAAAAHHHHH!"

"Um, what was that?" Rage asks.

"A scream," Aura says. "From outside. Hold on."

Then, she phases through the infirmary wall, and when she returns, her face is whiter than her normal ghostly self.

"Aura?" I ask. "What's wrong?"

"Z-Zombies," she says with a shaky voice. "There are Zombies all over campus."

CHAPTER TWELVE

ZOMBIEPOCALYPSE

Zombies?

There are Zombies on campus?

Then what Van Helsing said must be true. The Artifacts of Virtue do have Supernatural powers to ward off evil. And with the Bell of Virtue gone, we're sitting ducks!

My shoulders slump under my sense of guilt. After all, I was the one who opened the door that let Peter—Tiger-boy—inside the academy. If anyone gets hurt, it's all my fault.

I feel sick to my stomach.

"We've got to get out of here!" Aura says. "And we should take Cat-girl with us. I still don't believe she's as innocent as she claims."

"I believe her," I say. "If she and her brother were evil, they wouldn't have been able to step foot on school grounds in the first place because the Artifacts of Virtue would have kept them out. And based on her story, Dr.

Moreau didn't give them a choice. If they didn't steal one of the Artifacts of Virtue, they wouldn't get the antidote that could save their lives."

Aura and I stare each other down. I can tell she's thinking about what I said, but she's still not convinced.

"And by the way," Aura says. "I'm also questioning what side you're on."

For a second, her comment catches me off guard.

But then I realize I shouldn't be so surprised. I mean, I just admitted to committing an act of treason! But I couldn't let Kat take the blame for opening the vault door. I'm about to respond, when—

THOOM!

Suddenly, a green hand smashes through the wall!

"Zombies!" Rage yells.

"Take the girl and run!" Dr. Hagella commands, slamming the hand back through the wall with a fire extinguisher. "This is a sanctuary for the sick and injured, and if those zombies think they can destroy what we've built then they've got another thing coming."

Then, Dr. Hagella unhooks Kat from her IV and Rage and I help her to her feet. As she stands up, our eyes meet and I realize that underneath the whiskers and cat ears, she's really pretty.

"Um," I stammer. "Do you think you can run?"

"Like the wind," she says.

"Great," Rage says. "Let's go!"

"Students, get behind me," Dr. Renfield says,

bursting out the infirmary door onto the school grounds.

We follow close behind, and when I finally get outside, my eyes grow wide with horror, because there are dozens of zombies lumbering across campus. Their red eyes shine brightly through the night as they limp along aimlessly in packs of three of four.

"Don't let them bite you!" Aura calls out. "They'll turn you into a zombie!"

Roger that. I'm having enough trouble just being a vampire. The last thing I need is to become a vampire-zombie!

"Dr. Renfield!" Rage yells.

At the sound of his voice, I spin around to see two zombies grab Dr. Renfield's arms. But just as one opens his mouth, he's engulfed in a giant fireball and releases Dr. Renfield's arm! Then, Dr. Renfield kicks the other zombie in the midsection and pulls free just as that zombie goes up in flames.

Huh? How'd that happen?

But as the two zombies collapse to the ground I have my answer. Because Professor Hexum is standing behind them with his walking stick in one hand and a torch in the other.

"Thank you, Dr. Renfield, but I will take it from here," Hexum says. "I need you to go back to the auditorium immediately and help Professor Holmwood, Professor Seward, and Mrs. Clops relocate the other students. Mr. Murray's safety is now my concern."

Hexum's comments surprise me. I mean, why is he coming back here for me when so many other kids are in danger?

"B-But…" Dr. Renfield stammers, looking at me and then back at Hexum.

"Dr. Renfield," Hexum says firmly, "the Headmaster gave me full authority in his absence. Please go to the auditorium and help the others. That is an order and not a request."

"Of course," Dr. Renfield says finally. Then, he looks at me and says, "Take care of yourself, Mr. Murray. Hopefully, we will meet again."

I smile weakly as he heads off, but for some reason, his words strike me oddly.

"Let's go!" Hexum barks, grabbing my hoodie and pulling me forward.

"But, my friends," I say, digging my feet in to stop his momentum. "I can't just leave them."

Hexum turns to Aura, Rage, and Kat.

"Very well," he sighs, "come along."

"Yes!" Rage says, pumping his fist.

"Now move!" Hexum orders.

"Where are we going?" I ask.

But before Hexum can answer, we're suddenly surrounded by six more zombies!

"Get close to me!" Hexum commands.

But as we circle Hexum, even more zombies close in. Hexum waves his torch around us and in the blazing light

I can see the zombies' decaying faces. But Hexum's flame does its job, keeping the creatures at bay. If I wasn't about to die right now, I'd probably throw up.

"W-What now?" Rage asks.

That's when I notice he's breathing heavier.

Oh no.

If Rage loses control and turns into a purple sledgehammer, we'll have an entirely different problem on our hands. I need to keep him calm.

"Relax, buddy," I say, putting my hand on his shoulder. "We've got this. Don't we, Professor Hexum? Um, Professor Hexum?"

But when I look up, I notice his eyes are closed! He's focusing on something.

FWOOOMMM!

Suddenly, a giant ring of fire erupts all around us!

"Move forward!" Hexum barks.

At first, I resist. I mean, I don't want to walk straight into a raging fire. But Hexum pushes me forward, right into the zombies' path! But instead of getting burned, the ring of fire moves with us—keeping us safely in the center of its fiery circle!

As we charge ahead, the zombie crowd falls back, afraid of the fire blazing around us. And that's when I realize something else—there's no heat! If we were surrounded by an actual fire, we'd be incinerated instantly!

So, that can only mean one thing—it's an illusion!

Hexum must be using his mental powers to trick the simple-minded zombies into thinking this is a real fire—and I guess my simple mind as well. Within seconds, we've cleared a path through the zombie brigade and made our way off of school grounds through a hole in the busted perimeter wall. Then, Hexum turns and waves his arm, causing a massive wall of fire to flare up behind us.

There's no way they'll try crossing that.

Kat looks shell-shocked.

"W-What's happening?" she asks.

"Jedi mind tricks," I say.

"What now?" Aura asks. "What about our friends? Shouldn't we go back and save them?"

"No, it is too dangerous," Hexum says. "Besides, they are in good hands with the other teachers. There is an underground escape route from the auditorium that will take them safely off campus. But Mr. Murray is no longer safe here."

"So, where are we going to go?" Rage asks.

"Wait," Kat says sniffing the air. "It's Peter. I… I think I've picked up his scent. He went straight ahead. Through those woods."

"Excellent," Hexum says. "We can follow the trail."

"Hold on," Aura says. "Do you actually trust her? What if it's a trap?"

"I certainly hope it's a trap," Hexum says with a wicked smile. Then, he turns for the woods. "Let's go."

Aura frowns at me and then floats after Hexum.

Rage shrugs his shoulders and takes Kat by the arm, helping her along. But before I follow, I take one last look at our zombie-infested academy.

I can't imagine things getting worse, but deep down inside I have the dreadful feeling it will.

"Mr. Murray!" Hexum calls out.

"Coming!" I call back. Then, I flip my hood over my head and get moving.

***

It seems like we've been walking for hours. Every now and then, we cross a road or some train tracks, but other than that, it's been all woods all of the time. Hexum is still leading the way, which is pretty impressive since he needs a walking stick. Other than Aura, the rest of us look like we could collapse at any second.

Kat and I are a few paces behind Hexum. Once Rage tired out, I stepped in to help her over the rough terrain, but for a girl who just got out of a hospital bed, she's doing really well on her own. In fact, she seems to have no problem scampering over anything in our path.

"You're pretty agile," I say.

"Oh, thanks," she says, smiling at me. "I guess it's one of the perks of being part-cat. The tail not-so-much. I know I look freaky, but what's the story with your friends? I mean, that doctor had green skin like a witch. And if I didn't know better, I'd say that girl who doesn't like me is a ghost. And you look, well, sort of like—"

"—a vampire?" I say, finishing her sentence for her. "Yeah, well, that's because I am a vampire. Well, half-vampire anyway."

"And what about the blond kid?" she asks.

"You don't want to know," I say. "But I guess we all seem strange from your point of view. We didn't exactly explain things to you back in the infirmary. You see, our school is a school for monster kids."

"Monster kids?" she says.

"Yeah," I say. "That's us."

"Well, okay then," she says. "I guess that explains a lot. And by the way, thanks for stepping in about that vault door thing. Honestly, I didn't know what your friend was accusing me of."

"Oh, that's just Aura," I say. "Trust me, she's okay. Just give her some time. I'm sure she'll turn around. Well, I hope she'll turn around. Anyway, I'm sorry about what happened to you and your brother. It sounds like you've been through a lot."

"Yeah, thanks," she says. "He's a good person. I just wish he wasn't so impulsive all the time. That's why I feel like I need to keep an eye on him. I never know what he's going to get into—AH!"

Suddenly, Kat stops and doubles over. Based on her expression, it looks like she's in pain.

"Are you okay?" I ask, grabbing her shoulders so she doesn't topple over. "Professor Hexum, stop!"

"Y-Yes," she says, straightening up and leaning back. "Just got a sharp pain in my side."

"That's not good," Rage says, catching up to us. "Maybe you should sit down for a minute."

"N-No," she says, breathing heavily. "I don't want to lose Peter's scent. He's close. I can smell it. Let's just keep moving."

"Are you sure?" Hexum asks.

"Yes," she says.

Rage and I stand next to Kat and put one of her arms over each of our shoulders. As we start up again, I'm surprised by how light her body seems. It's like her bones are hollow or something.

"You know," Rage says. "the thing I can't figure out is why the Dark Ones would send zombies onto campus? I mean, if you wanted to destroy stuff, wouldn't you send werewolves?"

"That's simple," Aura says, floating beside me. "Most people think zombies are brainless, but in truth, they're just single-minded. If you give a zombie a goal, it will pursue that goal until it's destroyed. I think you need to brush up on your Monsterology."

"That makes sense," I say. "Remember when we went to the graveyard and those zombies were digging up those bones? I didn't think of it then, but I guess that's what they were told to do."

"Exactly," Aura says.

"Okay," Rage says, "so what do you think they were

looking for when they invaded our campus?"

"Bram, probably," Aura says. "Hexum said he wasn't safe there anymore."

"Great," I say, but just then something else pops into my head.

"What's wrong, Bram?" Aura asks. "Now you look like you've seen a ghost."

"What? Nothing." I say, "Except, Dr. Renfield told me there was something else on campus that Count Dracula was searching for. Something called the Spear of Darkness."

"Nonsense!" Hexum blurts out suddenly.

What's his problem? I didn't even realize he was listening to our conversation.

"That blowhard doesn't know what he's babbling about," Hexum continues. "The Spear of Darkness is not on campus and we will not discuss it any further."

Rage, Aura, and I exchange glances.

What's got him so riled up?

"What's the Spear of Darkness?" Rage mouths.

"Tell you later," I mouth back.

"Halt," Hexum says, blocking us with his walking stick.

Suddenly, I realize we're standing on the edge of a cliff. With all of the thick underbrush, I didn't even see the ground drop off. One wrong step from here and we could have tumbled hundreds of feet to our doom. Well, I guess this is a dead end. I start to turn back, when—

"There," Kat says, pointing across the way.

Huh? There? There where?

But when I follow her arm, I see an oddly shaped structure in the distance, peeking out from behind a tall mountain. It's not a rock formation or anything natural.

In fact, it kind of looks like… a tower?

"He's in there," Kat says. "My brother is in there."

CHAPTER THIRTEEN

DID YOU MIST ME?

As we stand at the cliff's edge, looking up at the dark tower randomly jutting out from the top of the mountain, there's only one thought running through my mind:

Nothing good ever happens in a dark tower.

And this one certainly fits the bill. It's tall and thin, rising from the mountainside like a twisted spire, its tip cutting through the full moon hanging behind it in the night sky. And as I scan the mountain itself, there's no obvious way to get up to the tower, other than scaling the mountain itself.

"Um, what is that thing?" Rage asks.

"Moreau's headquarters," Kat says. "That's where he took Peter and me. That's where he turned us… into this."

"M-Moreau?" Rage says with a shaky voice. "He's… in there?"

"Yes," Kat says. "I can smell his putrid cologne from here. He's in there. And so is my brother."

"Okay," I say. "Everyone stay calm for a minute.

Let's take Kat's word for it that they're both up there. That tower has a three-hundred-and-sixty-degree view of everything around it. I bet they can see for miles. There's no way anyone could sneak up on them."

"No," Hexum says. "But we are not just anyone. Students, please huddle."

"Alright," Aura says, rubbing her palms together. "I feel a plan coming on."

As Aura, Rage, and I circle Hexum, Kat stands on the cliff's edge.

"Now listen closely," Hexum says, gathering us all in with his walking stick. "If Katherine believes her brother is in that tower, then the Bell of Virtue is there as well. It must be retrieved to restore the academy's Supernatural protection from evil. But Moreau is a brutal adversary. He will not spare you simply because you are children. Therefore, this task is far too dangerous for your skill level. You will all wait here until I return."

"What?" Aura and I blurt out at the same time.

"Stop!" Rage adds, pointing at Hexum.

"Excuse me?" Hexum says, his eyebrows raised.

"No," Rage says, moving around Hexum and pointing down the cliff. "Stop her!"

Stop her? Stop who?

But when I turn around, Kat is gone! And that's when I see her climbing down the side of the cliff! While Hexum was talking to us, she took off on her own!

Is she crazy! Dr. Moreau will see her coming.

I've got to stop her!

Without a second thought, I picture myself as a bat and transform instantly. Then, I take flight.

"Bram, wait!" Aura yells, but I'm already soaring through the air.

"Mr. Murray, get back here at—!" Hexum yells, his voice fading in the distance.

I don't want to disobey him, but Kat is in real danger. At first, I don't see her, but then I pick her up using radar. She's already made it down to the base of the cliff and is bounding across the rocky surface towards the mountain. She's fast—maybe even faster than me—but I've got to catch her before we get—

AROOOOOOOOOOOOOO!

—spotted.

Uh oh. That sounded like a horn—otherwise known as an alarm—and it came from the top of the mountain! I glance back up at the cliff and Hexum, Rage, and Aura are gone. Hopefully, they're hiding back in the woods.

But that's more than I can say for Kat, because alarm or no alarm, she's not stopping. In fact, she's reached the bottom of the mountain and is starting to climb up! It's a long way to the top so this might be my only chance to stop her before Moreau sends who knows what army down to fight us.

But just as I swoop in, I hear—

FWOOP. FWOOP. FWOOP.

What's that?

Suddenly, I pick up something massive coming right at me through the air! Out of the corner of my eye, I catch a pair of giant wings, and I dart down just as it zooms over me, generating so much wind force it sends me into a tailspin! I flap my wings hard, pulling myself up before I crash onto the rocks below.

What the heck was that?

I loop around, but I don't see it anywhere. And what's even worse is I don't see Kat either! Did that thing get her?

"Psssst!" comes a voice. "Up here! Quick!"

I scan the mountain until I pick up a white speck waving at me from inside a cave. It's Kat! She's found a hideout in the side of the mountain! I've got to get to her and then get us out of here before—

SQUAWK!

I flap left as the creature nosedives past me!

Okay, that was way too close for comfort! But when I look down, I do a double take, because what's circling me is like nothing I've ever seen before. It's absolutely huge, with the head and wings of an eagle and the body of a lion! It's like some crazy person decided to stick two animals together just for laughs.

Except, in this case, the crazy person happens to be Dr. Moreau. But as it soars around me, I remember studying a beast like this in Monsterology class. I think it's called a griffin, and it's like facing two predators in one!

"Don't just sit there!" Kat yells. "Move!"

Well, I don't need to be told twice. The only problem is that the griffin isn't just going to just let me go. I beat my wings as hard as I can, heading for Kat, but there's no way I'm going to outrun this thing. I mean, its wingspan is like twenty feet long! I'm a bat snack!

It's coming!

Please, please somehow miss me.

Wait a second. 'Miss' me? 'Mist' me?

Suddenly, a lightbulb goes off.

I focus my concentration on becoming a mist.

But it's right behind me!

It's ten feet away.

Can't lose focus.

Five feet.

C'mon!

One foot.

Please.

Suddenly, my body feels weightless, and as the griffin flies through me, my molecules scatter everywhere.

Yes! I did it!

WAAAAAK!

I guess birdbrain is annoyed, but tough noogies, because I'm alive! All I need to do now is collect myself near Kat. It takes some doing in the open air, but I manage to gather my atoms over the ledge and transform back to a kid. As I hit the ground by her feet, I'm absolutely exhausted.

"Bram, move it!" Kat yells, running into a cave.

SQUUUAAAWWWKKK!

As the griffin's shadow covers the ledge, I follow her, squeezing through the narrow cave entrance. We go back as far as we can until we hit a dead end. Both of us lean against the rock wall, breathing heavily.

"Thanks for spotting me," I manage to say.

"I picked up your scent behind me," she says, her eyes wide. "But it took me a second to realize you were a bat. How did you do that?"

"Vampire, remember?" I say. "It's what we do. But enough about that. Do you think this cave opening is small enough?"

"For what?" she asks.

SQUAWK!

"That!" I say, pulling Kat back against the rock wall.

Just then, giant talons burst through the cave and claw around recklessly. But fortunately, the entrance is narrow enough to keep the griffin out. The beast pushes its shoulder against the opening to extend its reach, but it simply can't fit its body through.

"We're trapped," I say. "There's no way out."

"No," Kat says, sniffing into the air. "The smell."

"Sorry," I say. "I didn't exactly have time to put on deodorant."

"Not you," she says. "I've picked up Peter's scent again. He came this way. Follow me."

Then, she turns and climbs straight up the rock wall!

Where's she going now? I mean, I thought this was

literally a dead end. But to my surprise, Kat disappears through a hole in the rock ceiling.

"Come on!" she says, popping her head down through the hole. "There's a tunnel up here."

A tunnel?

I hate tunnels.

SQUAWK!

But as I look back at the cave opening, the griffin stretches its arm as far as it can and nearly shish kebobs me. Well, I haven't had the best of luck with tunnels, but it's got to be better than this.

"Coming!" I say, carefully scaling the rock wall.

When I reach the top, I pull myself through the opening and find Kat crouched low inside a narrow tunnel. That's strange. It seems to cut diagonally upwards through the mountain itself.

"Peter went this way," Kat says, heading through the tunnel.

I get to my feet and lean against the wall to catch my breath. I can't believe what's happened. I mean, just a little while ago we were all safe and sound at the Van Helsing Academy. Now I'm running through the mountain headquarters of a mad scientist.

I sure hope Rage and Aura got away before that griffin got them. And speaking of getting away, I've got to get moving to keep up with Kat, except I'm completely drained. I'd love to rest, but I can't let Kat face Moreau on her own. He's simply too dangerous.

"Come," a man's voice echoes through the cave.

Huh? Where'd that come from?

But when I look around, there's no one here but me.

"Come, Bram," he says.

That's when I realize the voice isn't echoing through the cave, it's echoing through my head! And what's worse is that I know who the voice belongs to.

Count Dracula!

I wait for him to speak again, but the only sound I hear is the beating of my own heart. Suddenly, I get chills. What exactly did he mean when he said 'come?' Is he here? Is he waiting to attack me?

I don't want to die.

"Bram?" Kat says, walking back towards me looking concerned. "Are you coming? I was calling you."

Suddenly, I'm confused.

Was that Kat calling me? But it didn't sound like her?

I want to tell her 'no,' I'm not coming. In fact, I'd rather take my chances with that hideous eagle-lion thing, but deep down I know I can't do that. She's not going to back down. I mean, her twin brother is in trouble. Plus, I'm responsible for what happened to the Van Helsing Academy. I'm the one who needs to find the Bell of Virtue or the school will be toast.

My mind must be playing tricks on me.

"Yeah," I say, pushing myself forward. "I'm coming. Sorry, I just needed a breather."

"It's okay," she says. "You've been through a lot.

Listen, I scouted ahead a bit and this tunnel just keeps going up and up. I think we're in some kind of a secret entrance to the tower."

"Dandy," I say. "Well, then, let's go for it."

She's about to turn, but then stops and freezes me with her bright, green eyes.

"I… I just want to say thanks again," she says. "I know we don't know each other that well, but I'm really glad you're here."

"Hey, no problem," I say, feeling my cheeks go flush. "I guess charging into highly terrifying situations is just what new friends do for each other."

She giggles and turns, brushing me with her tail, and then she takes off.

Well, here goes nothing.

I try keeping up with her, but it's difficult to match her agility navigating the twists and turns inside the tunnel. Considering that she could barely walk on her own when we left the infirmary, her cat-like adrenaline must be off the charts.

I hope she also has nine lives.

As we continue to weave our way along, my mind turns to other thoughts. Like, what happened to Van Helsing, Crawler, and Professor Morris? I mean, they went looking for Peter long before we started. And why was Dr. Renfield so reluctant to leave me when Hexum ordered him to go? And speaking of Hexum, why did he have such a big reaction when I mentioned the Spear of

Darkness?

Suddenly, I slam into Kat.

"Sorry," I say. "Why'd you stop?"

"Shhh," she whispers, her finger over her lips. "Look straight up."

And that's when I see it. I was so in my head I didn't even notice. We're crouched beneath a hatch door and there's light coming through the edges.

Dr. Moreau could be standing right over our heads!

"Okay," I whisper. "We need a plan. Let's—"

SMASH!

I flinch and shield my face as Kat bursts upwards through the hatch door!

And then I make a mental note:

Kat's not much of a planner.

MONSTEROLOGY 101 FIELD GUIDE

GRIFFIN

CLASSIFICATION:

Type: Abnormal

Sub-Type: Hybrid

Height: Variable

Weight: Variable

Eye Color: Red

Hair Color: Variable

KNOWN ABILITIES:

- Has the head, wings, and forelegs of an eagle and the hind-quarters of a lion
- Incredible strength, speed, and vision
- Large talons are razor -sharp

KNOWN WEAKNESSES:

- Lacks body armor
- Large size makes them easy to spot in the air
- Not intelligent

DANGER LEVEL:

HIGH

TIPS TO AVOID AN UNWANTED ENCOUNTER:

- Stay out of the air
- If outside, remain hidden under trees or beneath covered structures
- Avoid mountainous areas

CHAPTER FOURTEEN

PURE EVIL

And Kat said her brother is the impulsive one?

As I shield my body from the falling debris of the shattered hatch door, I realize I have no choice but to follow Kat into the mysterious room. This isn't how I would have approached the situation, but it's too late now. So, I stand up and pull myself through the opening.

And then I wish I hadn't done that.

We're standing in the center of a large, circular room with stone walls, large glass windows, and a high ceiling. Based on the sweeping three-hundred-and-sixty-degree view of the surrounding landscape, it's actually pretty cool up here. You know, if it weren't for the guy dressed in all white pointing the gun at us.

"Welcome," the man says. "Truthfully, I wasn't expecting you to survive my pet griffin, yet here you are."

Kat and I look at each other and freeze. Based on the terror in her eyes and her description from earlier, the guy doesn't need an introduction.

It's Dr. Moreau!

He's a bit older than I imagined, with white, slicked-back hair and deep wrinkles around his cold, gray eyes. His white, three-piece suit is pressed and pristine, and he's wearing a black tie and shiny, black shoes. But it's not his appearance that has my attention—not by a long shot. It's what he's holding in his left hand.

The Bell of Virtue!

"Looking for this?" he asks.

Well, yes. I want to tell him to hand it over, but the odds of him listening to me are zero to none. So, I hold my tongue. At least, for now.

"Where is Peter?" Kat demands. "You got what you wanted, now where is my brother?"

"Ah, yes," Dr. Moreau says. "They say twins have a special connection, don't they? Although you really don't look anything like twins anymore. A shame. I was so hoping you would evolve to be more like your brother."

"Where is he?" Kat repeats. "Tell me, you monster!"

"Insistent, aren't you?" Dr. Moreau says, placing the Bell of Virtue on a nearby table. "Have no fear, your savage brother is right here."

Then, he steps back and pulls a black cloth off a large box sitting behind him, revealing an iron cage with Peter inside! Peter is lying on his back, his stomach barely moving up and down.

"Peter!" Kat yells.

But just as she takes a step towards them, Dr. Moreau points his gun at the cage—right at Peter.

Kat stops cold.

"I suggest you stay there," he says. "After all, I would hate to waste a silver bullet on your poor brother. Especially since he is dying anyway."

Just then, Peter erupts in a deep coughing fit.

That's when I remember what Kat said. Dr. Moreau told them that neither of them had long to live. That they were the only ones who had even survived this type of transformation. But based on how bad Peter looks, I'm concerned his time could be running out.

"Give him the antidote!" Kat demands. "You promised that if we got you one of those Artifacts of Virtue, you'd give us the antidote. You have your stupid bell, now give it to him!"

"Ah, yes. The antidote," Dr. Moreau says, picking up a glass vial filled with a red liquid. "The only means of changing him back to natural form. Was this the antidote you were referring to?"

"Yes!" Kat says, her eyes growing wide. "That's it! Now give it to him! Please!"

But Dr. Moreau smiles.

And then he drinks it down in one gulp.

"No!" Kat yells.

"Foolish girl," Dr. Moreau says, wiping his mouth with his sleeve and putting the empty vial back on the table. "There is no antidote for your condition. There never was."

"Nooo!" Kat cries, dropping to her knees. "W-Why?

Why did you do this to us?"

"For this, of course," Dr. Moreau says, picking up the Bell of Virtue again. "With the Artifacts of Virtue in place, there was no way I could infiltrate the Van Helsing Academy myself. Instead, I needed to send in an agent. Someone with an innocent heart and a desperate mind who could pass through the school's magical protection, as long as they were properly motivated, of course. And when I discovered you and your brother digging for scraps in that back alley, I knew I had found my recruits."

"No," Kat says, as tears stream down her cheeks.

"But I still don't get it," I say. "You used them, but why? Why do you want to remove the school's magical protection in the first place?"

"For science," he says smugly.

"Um, what?" I say. "Sorry, but that makes no sense."

"It does to me," Dr. Moreau says. "You see, my brand of science has been deemed 'unacceptable' by mankind. And as a result, they have stripped me of my resources—my grants, my research, my laboratory. They took everything from me. And why? Because they are afraid of my genius."

Well, yeah, I can see why.

This guy is no genius. He's insane!

"It is human nature to fear what you do not understand," he continues. "And my former 'peers' failed to understand what I was striving to achieve. They said I was mad. They said it was morally wrong to create an entirely new species of Hybrid creatures merely to do the bidding of mankind. They said it couldn't be done, it shouldn't be done. Yet, I found a way to do it—to become the ultimate creator right here on earth."

Okay, this is going downhill fast.

"Despite all of their objections," Dr. Moreau continues, "all of their obstacles, I continued my work. However, they never accepted my arguments that a few must be sacrificed for the good of all. They tried to silence me, to cut me off, but I have persevered."

"Kat," I whisper, but she doesn't respond. She's just staring straight ahead, completely oblivious to everything happening around us.

"You see," he continues, "I am not like them. I am not limited by things like 'morals' or 'ethics.' Those beliefs only serve to restrain creativity. But I will not be stopped. And once I deliver my side of the bargain, I will be given all of the subjects I need to continue my genetic experiments, however, and wherever I please. I will have an army of Hybrids to follow my every command. And then I will show all of my adversaries what madness looks like."

Is that what this is all about? He's creating all of these Hybrid creatures, hurting all of these innocent people, just to serve his own ego? But then I remember something he said.

"Um, you mentioned something about a bargain," I say. "What are you talking about?"

"Observe," Dr. Moreau says.

Just then, a door on the far side of the room opens and two large men enter the room, except they're not men at all. They both have muscular, human bodies but animal heads! One has the head of an ox and the other the head of a bear, and I wonder if Dr. Moreau tricked them in the same way he tricked Kat and Peter?

But then I realize they're wheeling in two more covered boxes behind them, and the boxes are the same size as the one Peter is stuck in. Then, Dr. Moreau nods, and the beast-men whip off the cloth covers.

My jaw hits the floor.

It's Rage and Hexum!

Moreau's beast-men must have captured them after Kat and I took off. Poor Rage is gripping the iron bars and looking around with panic in his eyes. Hexum, however, is lying face down and not moving at all.

"Rage," I call out, "are you okay?"

"I-I think so," he answers.

"Professor?" I call out. "Are you okay?"

But Hexum doesn't answer.

"Do not worry," Dr. Moreau says. "He will be fine once he regains consciousness. At the moment he is enjoying a deep sleep."

I breathe a sigh of relief, but then I realize someone is missing. Where's Aura? I look around the room but don't see her anywhere.

"Let them go," I say firmly. "Now."

"I don't think so," Dr. Moreau says. "Professor Hexum's reputation precedes him and I really don't want to deal with his mind games. The boy, however, will make a fine specimen for one of my future experiments."

"W-What?" Rage says, his voice cracking. "B-But… you already experimented on me. Don't you remember?"

"I did?" Dr. Moreau says, studying Rage's face. "Funny, I don't remember you."

"B-But," Rage says meekly, looking stunned, "y-you ruined my life. And you don't even remember…"

"Please, child," Dr. Moreau says, shrugging his shoulders. "I experiment on dozens of specimens every day. It simply isn't important for me to remember them all. But enough of this. It is time to deliver what I promised. And then there will be no limit to my science."

I look over at Rage who is curling into a ball.

"Bring me the walking stick!" Dr. Moreau demands.

Wait, did he just say, 'walking stick?'

Like, as in Hexum's walking stick?

I'm totally confused as I watch the ox-man reach into Hexum's cage and yank out his walking stick. I mean, what does Dr. Moreau want with Hexum's walking stick? But as the burly beast-man hands it over to Dr. Moreau, the evil scientist breaks into a disturbing smile.

"My ploy worked brilliantly," he says, looking at the walking stick. "Truthfully, I never expected it to be this easy. But as luck would have it, my plan drove you from your academy and brought the prize right to my front door. I should probably thank you for your ignorance."

"What are you talking about?" I ask.

But Dr. Moreau doesn't answer me.

Instead, he walks over to a set of large windows and throws open the panes. Then, he raises the walking stick over his head.

"Come, my Dark Lord," he yells out the window. "Come to my tower and claim your bounty. For it is I, your most loyal servant, who will finally deliver what you have long been seeking. I willingly invite you to come inside, my King of Darkness!"

Um, did he just say, King... of Darkness?

A chill runs through my body.

"We've got to get everybody out of here!" I whisper to Kat, shaking her shoulders. "Now!"

"What?" she says finally. "What's happening?"

But before I can answer, a black mist flows through the open window and I know it's too late. It swirls around the room, passing over our heads, and then collects itself next to Dr. Moreau.

Holy cow! There's no mistaking it now!

"Yes, my Dark Lord," Dr. Moreau says, his face beaming.

I've got to stop this, but I'm pretty much on my own. I mean, Hexum and Rage are stuck in cages, Kat looks like a shell of herself, and Peter is dying. But I have to act. Lives are in danger!

I go with my best bet.

"Get up," I whisper to Kat, helping her to her feet. "We've got to work together."

But as soon as she stands up, things go from bad to worse, because the dark mist transforms into the one person I'd least like to invite to my birthday party.

Count Dracula!

"Um, is that…?" Kat whispers.

"Yep," I say. "The end of the world."

As I take him in, I'm shocked. He's incredibly tall, just like I remembered, but this time he looks… different. I mean, the last time I saw him he was struggling to breathe. But now, as he towers over Dr. Moreau, he looks, well, way healthier. His pale skin isn't paper-thin anymore and his black hair is thick and full. And when he sees me his red eyes flicker and he smiles—his white, pointed teeth gleaming inside his bright, red lips.

For some reason, I can't take my eyes off of him.

"Bram?" Kat whispers, nudging me in the arm. "Snap out of it."

I shake my head. She's right. That was weird. It almost felt like he had me in some kind of a spell.

"Got to… stay calm," I hear Rage mutter from inside his cage. "Need to… stay calm."

"My Dark Lord," Dr. Moreau says, presenting him with Hexum's walking stick, "here is the object you have long desired. Just as I have promised you."

"Thank you, my loyal servant," Count Dracula says, his voice much deeper than I expected. He takes the walking stick from Dr. Moreau and holds it out in front of him.

But I don't get it. What does Count Dracula want with Hexum's walking stick?

"You still don't see it, do you, young one?"

Wait, what?

That voice inside my head.

That sounded like… Count Dracula!

"You are seeing only what he wants you to see, but not what is truly here."

"What are you talking about?" I answer. *"And get out of my head!"*

"Your blood gave me life," he says. *"We are now bonded in ways you cannot even imagine. Forever."*

"No!"

"It is true," he says. *"But I see that you have not yet learned to use your powers to their full potential. Allow me to assist you. For your power to see the truth is not limited to when you are in bat-form. Try it now."*

My power to see the truth is not limited to when I'm in bat-form?

What's he talking about?

But then I get what he's saying. When I'm a bat, I can use radar to see things my human eyes can't detect.

But can I also do that when I'm not a bat?

I've never tried it before.

I focus in on Hexum's walking stick and activate my radar, sending high-frequency sounds at the object in

Count Dracula's hands.

And when it bounces back I'm stunned!

I mean, I had no clue I could use radar in human-form. That's incredible! But what's pinging back is even more incredible. Because according to my radar, the walking stick is much bigger than it looks. And one side ends in a long, sharp… point?

Suddenly, it hits me.

I-I can't believe it.

Hexum tricked us!

He never needed a walking stick.

In fact, his walking stick was never really a walking stick at all!

It's the Spear of Darkness!

CLASSIFIED

Person(s) of Interest

<u>CODE NAME:</u> NONE

<u>REAL NAME:</u> DR. SIMON MOREAU

<u>BASE OF OPERATIONS:</u> UNKNOWN

D.S.I.

<u>FACTS:</u> Dr. Moreau is a brilliant biologist renowned for pushing the boundaries of science. Lost all government funding when his experiments on people went beyond the scope of human morality. Escaped before his arrest and now his whereabouts are unknown.

<u>FIELD OBSERVATIONS:</u>

- Lacks morals and ethics
- Typically armed
- His "creations" usually die within days
- Observed meeting with known operatives of the Dark Ones organization

<u>Category:</u> Natural

<u>Sub-Type:</u> None

<u>Height:</u> 5'11"

<u>Weight:</u> 192 lbs

STATUS: ACTIVE TARGET

DEPARTMENT OF SUPERNATURAL INVESTIGATIONS

CHAPTER FIFTEEN

EVERYTHING GOES CRAZY

I'm speechless.

I mean, Hexum's walking stick wasn't ever a walking stick at all. It was the Spear of Darkness!

Hexum was fooling us with his mind powers this entire time. Now I understand why he flipped out when I mentioned the Spear of Darkness in the first place. Dr. Renfield was right, the Spear of Darkness was at the Van Helsing Academy, but it was hidden in plain sight!

And now that I've used my radar to expose the truth, I don't even see the walking stick anymore. Instead, I see a long, black spear with a sharp, black blade shimmering with the twinkling of a hundred tiny stars.

It's amazing to look at, but there's one problem.

It's in the hands of the one person everyone was trying to keep it away from.

"You see it now, don't you?" Count Dracula's voice says inside my mind. *"I can see it on your face."*

"We've got to get that away from him," I whisper to

Kat. "And fast."

But the question is how? I take a quick scan of my options. I've got Kat, but Peter is still in his cage looking worse for wear. Moreau isn't going to help us. Hexum is still knocked out. And Rage...

"B-Butterflies and puppies..." Rage says, breathing heavily inside his cage. "Just think of butterflies and puppies."

That's it!

"I need you to create a distraction," I whisper to Kat, "It's our only chance."

"Um, okay," she whispers back. "What kind of a distraction?"

"A big one," I whisper. "But be careful."

"Yeah, yeah," she whispers.

"Are you pleased, my Dark Lord?" Dr. Moreau asks.

"Yes, my loyal servant," Count Dracula answers, turning the spear in admiration. "I have searched for the Spear of Darkness for centuries, and now it is finally in my possession, where it belongs. According to ancient legend, once I throw the spear at the first rays of the morning sun, it will blanket the sky in eternal darkness, blocking all sunlight. Then, I will be free to walk the—"

"Yoohoo!"

"Who dares?" Count Dracula says, turning his head.

"Just furry little me," Kat says, running at incredible speed straight towards them. "You see, the old guy and I have some unfinished business."

Well, I have to give her credit, she certainly knows how to create a distraction. But I can't just stand here gawking, I've got a job to do. Mustering up my own super-speed, I rush over to Rage's cage before the beast-men can react.

"Butterflies," Rage mutters, his face bright red. "Stay calm. Gotta... stay calm."

I feel guilty for what I'm about to do, but I know I have no choice. For everyone's sake.

"Dude," I whisper. "This isn't stay calm time. This is crush the butterflies and puppies time. I mean, you heard what Dr. Morcau said. He doesn't even remember you. He has no recollection of what he did to you. But you can make him remember. You can show him what happens when you get angry. Just let yourself go."

"A-Angry?" Rage says, his breathing quickening. "Make him... remember me? Let myself... go?"

"Yes," I say. "Show him what you've become. Show him what he did to you."

"I-I'll show him," Rage says, the veins popping out of his neck. "C-Crush butterflies. C-Crush puppies."

"Back off!" Dr. Moreau yells.

His scream grabs my attention, and that's when I see Kat jumping on top of Moreau! Uh-oh. I told her to be careful. I mean, Moreau's got a—

BLAM!

There's a blinding flash of white light.

"Aaahhh!" Kat yells.

And when she hits the ground she rolls over in pain, holding her right arm! She's been shot!

"GRRRRRAAARRR!" Peter growls from his cage.

I've got to stop the bleeding! But just as I start to move, the two beast-men pull me back!

"Get off of me!" I yell. "Let! Me! G—"

RRRIIIPPP! CCCLLLAAANNNGGG!

Suddenly, metal bars fly past my head, and something slams into Ox-man with such force that he knocks us all to the ground. As we hit the deck I narrowly avoid being crushed by the bear-headed guy when everything darkens around us.

And when I look up, my jaw drops.

Because standing over us is a seven-foot, purple monster with blond hair, ginormous muscles, and a really, really angry expression.

Yes!

It worked! Rage became a monster!

But, oh no!

If I can't control him, he'll destroy everyone in this chamber—including the good guys!

"Rage?" I call out.

Rage looks around the room and then spots me lying by his feet.

Uh oh.

"RRROOOAAARRRR!"

My hair blows straight back, and I just manage to roll out of the way as Rage reaches down and picks up Ox-man who howls in protest. But Rage ignores his pleas and throws him hard against the wall. Ox-man flops onto the floor and doesn't get back up.

"Is that purple monster one of your creations, Moreau?" Count Dracula asks. "Stop it. Before it ruins everything."

"I-I can't believe it," Dr. Moreau stammers, staring at Rage. "It can't be…."

"Moreau?" Count Dracula says. "Do something!"

Moreau! That's right!

"Rage, over there!" I yell, pointing at Dr. Moreau. "He's the one you want! He's the one who did this to you! He's the one who turned you into a monster!"

Rage studies me for a moment and then looks over at Dr. Moreau who raises his gun.

BLAM!

I turn away as the bullet whizzes past me and ricochets off of Rage's chest, lodging into the rafters.

"RRROOOAAARRR!!!" Rage yells.

Then, with surprising speed, Rage picks up Bear-man and hurls him right at Dr. Moreau.

BLAM!

The gun goes off again as they tumble to the floor.

"Aargh!" Count Dracula yells, dropping the Spear of Darkness to the ground. He's shaking his left hand, which is smoking, but there's no blood. "You careless fool!"

He's hit! This is my chance!

I turn on my super-speed, scoop up the Spear of

Darkness, and race over to Kat. When I reach her, she's lying on her side, wincing in pain.

"Kat, are you okay?"

"I-I think so," she says. "Just stings. And losing blood. Need… a doctor."

She's right. Her arm is bleeding—a lot—and for a second I freeze. I mean, her blood could reenergize me.

Wait, no! What am I thinking?

That's not me talking. I've got to snap out of it. I've got to help her. I pull off my hoodie and wrap it tightly around her forearm. That might help stop the bleeding for a while.

Now, if I can just get her out of here before—

STOMP!

Rage's footstep bounces us in the air like popcorn kernels, and when I look up I see him heading our way!

His brow is furrowed and he's focused on one target.

Dr. Moreau.

"No!" Dr. Moreau says, scrambling to find his gun. "Stop him! My Dark Lord, please, save me!"

"I am afraid this is your affair," Count Dracula says, wrapping himself in his cloak and disappearing into a black mist.

"You!" Dr. Moreau says desperately, turning to Peter. "Help me!" Then, he reaches inside his jacket pocket, pulls out a key, and fumbles to unlock Peter's cage. "Destroy that monster and I'll give you the real antidote. I promise you."

"GRRRRRR," Peter snarls, limping out of his cage. But he doesn't look fit enough to fight anybody. His whole head is nearly bald and he's leaning hard to his right like he's going to fall over.

"RRRAAARRRGGGHHH!" Rage roars, towering over Peter.

Oh, jeez. Rage is gonna pummel Peter!

"N-No, Peter!" Kat yells from her position. "D-Don't listen to Moreau! He lied to us! S-Save yourself!"

"Ignore her, Tiger-child," Dr. Moreau says, backing up behind Peter towards the open window. "You're dying. Without me, you won't last until morning. I have the real antidote. I can save you... and your sister too. Don't you want to save her?"

But then Dr. Moreau bends over.

And that's when I see it.

"The gun!" I yell. "He's going for his gun!"

Suddenly, Peter wheels around and lunges at Dr. Moreau. They grapple for a second before Peter lifts the evil scientist into the air and over his shoulder.

"Release me!" Dr. Moreau yells.

But Peter jumps onto the windowsill with Dr. Moreau in his arms. Then, he looks out the window.

"Peter, no!" Kat yells.

Peter turns and stares at his sister for a second, his eyes wide. And then he falls backward out the window, taking the squirming Dr. Moreau with him.

"Noooooooo!" Dr. Moreau yells, his voice fading in

the distance.

"No!" Kat yells. "Peter!"

I race over to the window and look down, but they're gone. We must be a hundred feet in the air! I-I can't believe it. Peter pulled Dr. Moreau down to his death. He sacrificed himself for us.

"RRRROOOOAAARRRR!"

Speaking of death…

I turn around slowly to find Rage standing over me, looking out the window himself. What is he doing? And that's when I realize what's happening. Peter robbed Rage of his chance for revenge. Rage wanted a shot at Dr. Moreau, but now he'll never get it.

"GGGRRRRAAAARRRR!" Rage yells.

Um, oh boy.

"MMAAKKE! HHIIMM! RREMMEMMBBERR!"

"Mr. Murray!" comes a familiar voice. "Move!"

I dive out of the way just as Rage jumps out of the window, taking half of the wall down with him!

"Rage!" I yell. "No!"

"Do not worry," the voice says. "He will be fine. He is nearly indestructible."

At first, I'm confused as to who's talking to me. But when I turn around I see Hexum moving inside of his cage. He's awake!

"Look out!" Hexum yells, pointing up high.

Suddenly, a huge bat drops from the rafters and latches onto the Spear of Darkness! It's Count Dracula!

With everything going on, I forgot all about him! How could I be so dumb!

I hold onto the spear with everything I've got, but I'm not strong enough, and Dracula flaps his mighty wings, ripping it clean from my grasp.

No!

But before I can stop him, he flies out the window!

I can't let him get away! The world is in danger!

Out of the corner of my eye, I spot the Bell of Virtue. In all of the commotion, it's been forgotten. But I guess it was only a means to an end anyway. Count Dracula has what he wanted all along.

"Kat," I say quickly. "I know you're hurting right now, but you've got to let Professor Hexum out of his cage. He can help you. And Professor, don't forget to bring the Bell of Virtue back to the school! The other kids will be safe."

"Mr. Murray—Bram—wait!" Hexum yells. "It is too dangerous!"

Hearing Hexum use my first name stops me cold, and I look into his concerned eyes. He's right, it is dangerous, but it's my responsibility to stop Count Dracula.

So, I focus my mind on one thought—becoming a bat—and then I transform. My arms shrink and then expand into wings, my legs retract into my body, and my senses explode.

And then I fly out the window.

CHAPTER SIXTEEN

TWO BATS OF A FEATHER

I spot Count Dracula against the purple sky.

Fortunately, given his sheer size, he's pretty hard to miss. He's flying away from the tower, still holding the Spear of Darkness in his feet. But there's something strange about how he's flying. He's tilted a little to the left like he's wounded.

At this point, I'm absolutely exhausted, but I can't stop now. Dracula may be faster and stronger, but I can't let him get away with the Spear of Darkness. I need to give it my all to stop him, even if it costs me my life.

I put everything I've got into flapping, but my wingspan is no match for his. I mean, his wings must be seven feet wide when fully extended! But if I can't out-flap him, maybe I can outsmart him.

Changing my trajectory, I go for height over distance, reaching an altitude higher than he's flying at. Then, I tuck in my wings and use gravity to my advantage, dive-bombing right at him.

As the wind whips across my bat-face, I realize I

don't exactly have a plan when I reach him. Should I try knocking him out or should I go for the Spear of Darkness? And what happens if I miss? I mean, we're hundreds of feet above the ground, so if I mess up it could be a long way down.

Decisions, decisions.

He's five feet away!

Since all I see is his back, I know what I've got to do.

Three feet!

I aim for his spine.

One foot!

I brace for impact, but just when I expect to make contact, there's nothing. What happened? But I'll have to figure that out later because I'm hurtling straight down.

I'm gonna crash!

I start flapping as hard as I can and pull myself up, my toes scraping the top of the rocks below. Whew! That was a close one. But as I pull back up, I find Count Dracula hovering above me.

"Why are you fighting me?" Count Dracula asks, his voice echoing in my brain. *"After all, we are the only two vampires on the planet. Why not join me instead?"*

"Um, what?" I say in my mind.

"Once the sun rises," he says, *"and I use the Spear of Darkness to put out its light forever, the Earth will be shrouded in eternal darkness. I will be unstoppable."*

"No!" I yell back. *"I won't let that happen!"*

"You cannot stop me," Count Dracula says. *"It is bad*

enough that you do not know how to harness the full extent of your power, but your greatest weakness lies in your naivete."

"What are you talking about?"

"You may think you are safe under the house of Van Helsing," he says, *"but you are wrong. The Van Helsing bloodline carries one goal and one goal only—the complete and utter destruction of all vampires. Think into the future. Once he is finished using you to destroy me, what fate will befall you as the last remaining vampire?"*

As I stare into his red eyes, I feel like I've been punched in the gut. I mean, what if he's right? What if Van Helsing is only using me to destroy Count Dracula? If I'm the last vampire left, what will Van Helsing do with me after that?

"Abraham Murray, you are what you are for a reason," he says. *"You may try to fight it, but your vampire tendencies are slowly taking over your body—taking over your soul. You can only fight it for so long before you will have to give in."*

H-How does he know that?

"Join me," he continues, *"and I will show you what it means to be a vampire. Join me and fulfill your true destiny. Join me and we will rule over mankind."*

Strangely, I-I feel myself being pulled to him. But then the faces of my friends flash through my mind.

Aura. Rage. Stanphibian. Hairball. InvisiBill—not that I can even see his face.

"No!" I yell, snapping back to reality. *"I-I'm not like*

you! I'll never be like you."

"A pity," he says. *"Because that means I must destroy you."*

Then, he rotates the Spear of Darkness with his feet, pointing the sharp blade right at me! And that's when I notice his left wing is smoking! That was the spot where Dr. Moreau accidentally shot him. He must have used a silver bullet. No wonder he was flying off-kilter.

But silver bullets will only wound a vampire's mortal body They won't destroy its spirit. According to Van Helsing, only a vampire can truly kill another vampire— spirit and all.

"Farewell," Count Dracula says, coming towards me.

Holy cow! I start flapping backward, but he's coming too fast. I'm a goner!

SSSQQQUUUAAAKKK!

Suddenly, a giant winged creature swoops past my field of vision, taking Count Dracula with it!

The force of the wind gust propels me backward, and I flap like crazy to stop my momentum before I hit the rocks below.

After righting myself, I look up into the sky to find the griffin soaring above, with Count Dracula in its mouth! But that doesn't last for long, because one second later the beast is chomping on nothing but a dark cloud.

Count Dracula escaped!

But then I see something else.

The Spear of Darkness is falling to earth!

I've got to grab it! Then, a lightbulb goes off. Dracula said I didn't know the full potential of my power. So, if I can use my radar power in human form, then maybe I can use my super speed in bat form?

I concentrate and then flap, turning on the jets, and the next thing I know, I'm off like a rocket! I grab the spear in mid-air and circle. Now I've got to get out of here before I get killed, or even worse, eaten! But as I try to use my speed again, I can't. I'm plum out of gas!

Just then, I sense I giant object flying over me. It's the griffin! And out of the corner of my eye, I see a large bat heading my way!

At this pace, we're all gonna collide into each other!

Where's an air-traffic controller when you need one?

I try flapping but it's no use. I've got nothing left in the tank and I'm losing altitude. There's no way I can outrun them. My only option is to turn into a mist—if I can even do that. But if I do, I may have to release the Spear of Darkness! I don't know if I'll be able to carry something so large in mist form.

I don't know what to do.

They're almost on me!

I feel like I'm gonna pass out.

I close my eyes.

THWIP!

SSSQQQUUUAAAKKK!!!

Huh? What was that ear-piercing scream?

But when I look up I see a silver arrow sticking out

of the griffin's chest, and then it plummets down, barreling into Count Dracula on its way!

Where'd that arrow come from?

"Bram!" a girl's voice calls.

What? Who?

But as I scan the ground below, I find a transparent girl floating off the ground. And next to her are three men, one of whom has spider legs, and another is pointing a crossbow my way.

It's Aura! And that's Van Helsing, Crawler, and Professor Morris! They found us!

Just then, the griffin CRASHES to the ground, kicking up a giant pile of feathers.

But there's no sign of Count Dracula.

Suddenly, the sky brightens and my body feels warm. It's the sun! It's coming up! And that's when I realize that if I stay up here, I'll get a really, really bad sunburn.

Not that I can maintain this height anyway. I'm wiped, and the Spear of Darkness is getting heavier by the second. Everything is getting dizzy.

And then I drop like an anchor.

"Bram!" I hear Aura yell. "Turn into a mist!"

Yeah.

Good idea.

Is that the ground?

Why is it spinning like that?

"Bram, drop the spear!"

Spear? Right. I open my toes.

"—mist!" Aura yells.

What was that?

Mist.

Right.

***

"Bram?"

I hear a voice, but it's so dark.

"Bram, wake up."

I try opening my eyes, but they feel super sticky.

"Bram?"

"Trying," I say.

And then, with what seems like Herculean effort, I manage to pry my eyes open. There's a bright light overhead, and a smiling, blue-eyed girl hovering over me.

"Am I dead?" I ask, squinting in the light.

"Almost," Aura says. "I'd say you tried really hard. But no, you're not dead."

"Oh," I say. I try sitting up, but my whole body hurts. "Where am I?"

"In the infirmary," Aura says. "You're back home."

Home? I look down at my arm and there's an IV stuck in it running red fluids into my body. It feels amazing. But I can't quite figure out how I got here in the first place. I remember something about a spear. And a bell. And—

"Rage!" I say, popping up, causing the monitors to

go bonkers. "And Kat! Where are they? Count Dracula is on the loose and—"

"Relax, Bram," Aura says. "Settle down. Rage is just fine. And Kat is too. They're getting care also. Everything is okay. Well, mostly okay."

"Glad to see he's alert," Dr. Hagella says, entering the room and quieting the monitors. "There are a few visitors here who are waiting to see you."

That's when I notice the infirmary has a bunch of holes in the wall. And then I remember the zombie attack. Dr. Hagella must have held them at bay after all.

Boy, she is one tough lady.

"W-What happened?" I ask. "The last thing I remember is stealing the Spear of Darkness from Count Dracula and freefalling. After that, it's pretty much a blank."

"Well," Aura says, "it's kind of a long story."

"I can handle it from here," comes a familiar voice from the doorway. "Can you give us some time alone?"

It's Van Helsing! I remember him saving me with the Crossbow of Purity. I'm happy to see him, yet something inside of me is telling me to be wary. Like I can't fully trust him.

"Of course, Headmaster," Aura says. "Feel better, Bram." And then she smiles at me and phases through the wall.

"You are lucky to have such a caring friend," Van Helsing says, sitting on the edge of my bed.

"Yeah," I say. "She's pretty awesome."

"Yes, in more ways than one," Van Helsing says. "Once Rage and Professor Hexum were captured, she went in search of us and found us on the far end of the forest. Fortunately, we got to you in the nick of time."

"No wonder she wasn't around," I say.

"Indeed," Van Helsing says. "How do you feel?"

"Like I've been run over by a truck," I answer.

"You have had quite an adventure," Van Helsing says. "Much of which seemed outside of your control."

What's he talking about? And then I realize he's referring to the episode in the tunnel. We never did resolve my punishment for that. Is that why he's here now?

"Tell me, Bram," he says, "were there other moments you have felt out of control? Is there anything you are not telling me?"

His question catches me off guard. I open my mouth to speak, but nothing comes out. I mean, I still haven't told him about nearly sucking Rage's blood at Moreau Labs. And then there was the situation with Kat's wound. I want to tell him about it, but then my conversation with Count Dracula comes flooding back.

No wonder I feel on edge. What if Count Dracula was right? What if Van Helsing is only using me?

"Um, no," I say, rather unconvincingly. "You know everything I know."

"Are you sure?" Van Helsing asks, raising his

eyebrows. "For example, I only recently learned from your peers that you were hypnotized by Dr. Renfield. Do you remember that?"

Dr. Renfield? That's funny. With everything going on, I totally forgot about him. He was the one who brought up the Spear of Darkness in the first place.

"Yes," I say. "But he was just making an example of me because I passed a note in his class."

"It may have seemed that way at the time," Van Helsing says, "but I believe he was doing much more than that. And now he is nowhere to be found."

"What?" I say. "You mean, he's gone?"

"Yes," Van Helsing says. "He never met up with the others in the auditorium."

"So," I say, trying to put the pieces together, "what exactly are you telling me?"

"What I am saying is that I made a mistake," Van Helsing says. "I believe Dr. Renfield did more than just hypnotize you that day. I believe he put subtle instructions inside your mind to sneak into the forbidden basement and open that vault door. You see, I now believe Dr. Renfield is working for the Dark Ones. He was looking for the Spear of Darkness."

"Excuse me?" I blurt out.

"I know it is shocking to hear," Van Helsing says. "But I put it all together once Professor Hexum told me about Dr. Renfield's comments regarding the Spear of Darkness. As a master of hypnosis, it was easy for him to execute once he had you in a trance. Although it appeared he was asking you simple questions, he was actually implanting detailed instructions deep in your mind. And none of the other students were any the wiser. That is why you have little memory of going into the forbidden basement and opening the vault door. You were in an unconscious state, almost like sleepwalking. And you followed his instructions perfectly."

Now I'm in total shock. I feel like such a fool. But it's no wonder I did what I did. I was manipulated!

"After Crawler subdued Rage," Van Helsing says, "I sent him after Dr. Renfield. But it is likely too late."

"And what happened to the Spear of Darkness?" I ask. "Does Count Dracula have it?"

"No, it is safe," Van Helsing says, "thanks to you. Professor Hexum did a good job disguising it for a long, long time. But now that its hiding place has been discovered, I have taken it back into my possession. I am the only person who knows where it is."

"And the Bell of Virtue?" I ask.

"It has also been returned to its proper place," Van Helsing says. "Professor Hexum and Katherine brought it back from the tower. The school is safe once again under the protection of the Artifacts of Virtue. And I have removed all known hidden entrances to the academy. The vault door and basement entry are gone."

Well, that's a relief.

But that's not the only thing I'm worried about.

"But what about Count Dracula?" I ask. "He got away, didn't he?"

"He did," Van Helsing says. "He escaped before sunrise. If we had only kept him exposed to the sunlight for a while longer, we at least would have destroyed his mortal body. But alas, it was not meant to be."

Well, that would have been great. I'd take destroying Count Dracula's mortal body any day of the week. At least it would buy me some time before I had to deal with his spirit.

"Your friends are excited to see you," Van Helsing says. "But I have one last question. When we arrived on the scene, I noticed that you and Count Dracula faced each other in bat-form for a long while without fighting. What was happening?"

Suddenly, my mind starts spinning. I mean, what am I supposed to say? Should I tell him that Dracula wanted me on his side? Or that he told me not to trust Van Helsing? I mean, what if Count Dracula was right? What if Van Helsing doesn't want any vampires alive at the end of all of this.

"Um, nothing much," I say finally. "He was just crowing about how powerful he was and that he wanted me dead. You know, the usual stuff."

Van Helsing squints and smiles at me.

He doesn't believe me for a second.

"Very well," he says, patting my arm. "You have done well, Bram. I am proud of you."

"Thanks," I say.

"Now let me bring in your friends," Van Helsing says. "They have some news to share."

"Okay," I say, as Van Helsing stands up and exits.

Then, Aura returns, with Hairball, Stanphibian, and InvisiBill in tow—or at least I think InvisiBill is in tow.

"Hey, Brampire," Hairball says. "Are you okay?"

"Yeah," I say, lying through my teeth. "I'm great."

"Awesome," InvisiBill says, his voice booming from the foot of my bed. "Because you'll never guess what Professor Hexum just did."

EPILOGUE

STARTING OVER

"**A**re you sure you're ready for this?" Rage asks.

"I was born ready," I answer with a smile, looking at all of the teams gathered in the gymnasium. It's been a few weeks since the incident at Moreau's tower, and I'm feeling much better.

"I never thought we'd get back in the Monster Cup," Rage says. "I thought we were done for good."

Honestly, so was I. But I was thrilled when the team told me that Professor Hexum reversed his disqualification ruling. I mean, I know how much the team wanted to win the cup.

Heck, I kind of wanted to win it too.

And now we'll actually have the chance.

With everything that happened after the Bell of Virtue was stolen, the competition never got off the ground, so Van Helsing decided to restart the entire tournament once the school was patched up. For the first time, as a signal of school solidarity, he's having all of the teams compete in each event at the same time.

And the first race is about to begin!

"Listen, Bram," Aura says. "We're all sorry for the way we treated you when we got kicked out of the Monster Cup. And we're not just saying that because we're back in the competition. Can you ever forgive us?"

"Can I forgive you guys?" I say. "Of course I can. I mean, after everything I did, I'm wondering if you can forgive me?"

"You're totally forgiven," Aura says.

"Not so fast," InvisiBill says. "Let's see if he wins his heat first."

"Shut it, InvisiBill," Hairball says.

"Break a wing," Stanphibian grunts.

"Thanks," I say. "I will."

We all put our hands in a circle and on the count of three yell, "Monstrosities!"

It feels great having the gang back together. And I'm so relieved I'll have the chance to make it up to them. But before my race begins, I need to check on one more person.

"Is everything ready?" I whisper to Aura.

"Yep," she whispers. "Would you like to do the honors?"

I nod and then walk over to the bleachers where I find Kat sitting with her arm in a cast.

"How are you doing?" I ask.

"Okay," she says. "Except for this, of course. Dr. Hagella said the bullet shattered my radius bone. I guess the good news is that I should heal pretty fast due to my cat anatomy."

"Well, that's great news," I say. "Kat, I'm so sorry about your brother. You were right, he had a good heart."

"Thanks, Bram," she says, looking down and wiping away a tear. "I'll miss him forever."

"He did a brave thing," I say. "And he did it to protect you."

"Yeah, I know," she says. "He was the best."

"So," I say, "Van Helsing told us he invited you to stay here at the academy."

"Yeah," she says. "It was nice of him to offer. I mean, I don't exactly have anywhere else to go, especially looking like this. So, I guess I'm stuck with you guys now."

"Well, I'd be thrilled if you stayed," I say. "We could use someone with your skills. You're an animal out there. Literally."

We both look at each other and laugh.

"Well, what about your friends?" she says. "I don't know if they want me here. Especially your ghost friend."

"Don't worry," Aura says, appearing behind her. "Of course I want you here. You've more than proven yourself to me, and we need all the help we can get."

"Really?" Kat says.

"Really," Aura says. "Fish-face, give her the gear."

Just then, Stanphibian walks up and hands her a black sweater and a silver badge.

"Welcome to the Monstrosities," Aura says.

"Are you serious?" Kat asks, breaking into a big smile. Then, she picks up the badge, turns it over, and reads the name engraved in its center. "WildKat?"

"That's your new code name," I say. "And after seeing the way you fight, it's well earned."

"Thanks," she says, holding the badge against her heart. "You know, you guys are great."

"Racers, please report to the starting line!" Hexum calls into a megaphone.

"Well, that's me," I say.

"Good luck, Bram," Kat says.

"You've got this," Rage says.

"If you lose, you're still a moron!" InvisiBill adds.

Yep, it's good to see things are back to normal.

As I approach the starting line, I notice Professor Hexum is no longer pretending to use a walking stick. Now that Van Helsing has the Spear of Darkness, I guess there's no reason to keep up the charade.

"Mr. Murray," Hexum says, casually acknowledging my presence like the whole crazy tower episode never even happened.

"Professor," I say, acknowledging him back. "Before we start, I want to thank you for allowing us to compete."

"Kindness will not earn you any extra advantages,"

Hexum says. "You will win or lose based on your own merits."

Yep, things are definitely back to normal.

"Get ready to eat my dust, loser," Harpoon says, lining up next to me.

"The only thing I'll be eating is victory cake," I answer back with a wink.

"We'll see about that," she grumbles.

Well, I know one thing. This isn't going to be easy. I mean, all of the best flyers are in this race. But if I use what Count Dracula taught me about combining my abilities, I should give them all a run for their money.

"Racers, on your mark!" Hexum calls out.

Aura and Kat give me a thumbs up.

"Get set!"

Then, I catch Van Helsing staring at me from the stands. He nods and I wonder if he still trusts me.

But what's even worse is that I'm starting to wonder if I trust myself.

"Go!"

For a split second, I hesitate as everyone else takes off. And then I transform into a bat and take flight.

THE
MONSTROSITIES

———

MONSTER CUP
XLII
CHAMPIONS

GET MONSTER PROBLEMS 3!

Count Dracula's war against humanity has officially begun and Bram must stop the King of Darkness once and for all, even if it costs him his life! But is Bram really ready to face the greatest evil of all time? And can he stop himself from turning into a full-fledged vampire?

Read Monster Problems 3 Today!

YOU CAN MAKE A BIG DIFFERENCE

Calling all monsters! I need your help to get Monster Problems 2 in front of more readers.

Reviews are extremely helpful in getting attention for my books. I wish I had the marketing muscle of the major publishers, but instead, I have something far more valuable, loyal readers just like you! Your generosity in providing an honest review will help bring this book to the attention of more readers.

So, if you've enjoyed this book, I would be very grateful if you could leave a quick review on the book's Amazon page.

Thanks for your support!

R.L. Ullman

DON'T MISS EPIC ZERO!

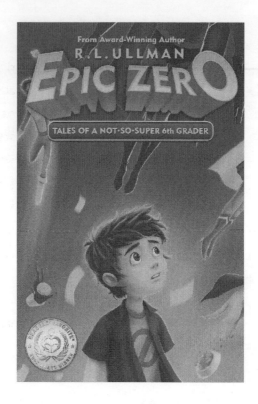

Growing up in a superhero family is cool, unless you're powerless...

Gold Medal Winner - Readers' Favorite Book Awards

Epic Zero: Tales of a Not-So-Super 6th Grader is the first book in a hilarious, action-packed series that will entertain kids, middle school students, and adults!

ABOUT THE AUTHOR

R.L. Ullman is the bestselling author of the award-winning EPIC ZERO series and the award-winning MONSTER PROBLEMS series. He creates fun, engaging page-turners that captivate the imaginations of kids and adults alike. His original, relatable characters face adventure and adversity that bring out their inner strengths. He's frequently distracted thinking up new stories, and once got lost in his own neighborhood. You can learn more about what R.L. is up to at rlullman.com, and if you see him wandering around your street please point him in the right direction home.

For news, updates, and free stuff, please sign up for the Epic Newsflash at rlullman.com.

***

As always, I would like to thank my Supernatural wife, Lynn, and my freakishly creative kids, Matthew and Olivia, for their undying support.

Made in the USA
Columbia, SC
28 July 2020